# WARZONE

## Anne Olivant

eISBN: 978-1-9997842-1-8
ISBN: 978-1-9997842-0-1

Typesetting by Robert Harries for Head & Heart Book Design

# WARZONE

*To Emily, Isaac, Lucy, Charlotte and Caspian*
*May you all grow up brave*

# PROLOGUE

A young knight galloping an old horse at the tilt. Buzzards in the air and a patient border collie, waiting to go home. These were the scenes that made up my world.

Until the day my world changed.

I was younger then, twelve years old. The only thing on my mind was getting my 'advance and lift' perfect in my new passion of jousting. Two months earlier, in history, I had learned for the first time about knights and jousting from a book about medieval riding contests.

'Please let me have a go with Oscar,' I'd begged Mum and Dad. My slightly fat, piebald cob Oscar had retired from most of the heavy work by then but really needed something to do instead of eating grass.

'He's such a good boy and I'm sure he would be easy to train.'

Dad had winked at Mum. I took that as a challenge and started immediately.

Mum always impressed me by the amount of stuff she knew, but especially now; what she seemed to know about trick riding was impressive.

'I was well into jousting and stuff at your age,' was all she admitted. 'And we don't forge chainmail this century, we knit it.' So out came the knitting needles. While Oscar and I practised she sat and knitted. 'Rather like the old women at the guillotine in the French Revolution,' she joked.

I often wondered how the knights managed when the helmets were made of heavy steel and the chainmail wasn't knitted. My hair, black and very curly, was always getting tangled up in the helmet, a papier-mâché thing that fitted over my riding hat.

'I don't think they used damsels for jousting and I guess the knights shaved their heads,' my dad said, drily. They wouldn't let me have mine shaved, but I had it as short as Dad's and that was much better.

My horse Oscar had surprised me too. He seemed to know what I wanted before I did and his accuracy and agility astounded me. I'd thought him a lazy old plodder. Now he was an enthusiastic forward-going warhorse!

That day we were going to gallop in a straight

line, without tripping or me falling off. With my 'lance' – a long bean pole – I was going to lift the 'lady's favour' – a red neckerchief – from 'my lady' – in this case, from the back of Vince, my long suffering border collie.

We had tried this so many times before, with as many results: falling off, dropping the lance, or missing the neckerchief by miles. But we had to do it that day. Dad had promised me a proper trick-riding saddle from the saddler at the St Peter's Fair next day. But only if we were perfect.

We thundered down the field to where Vince lay, motionless in the grass. I held the lance firmly at the horizontal, one end wedged in my armpit. At the last moment, Oscar swerved slightly. I dropped the point of the lance, and hooked the neckerchief up and away. As I shrieked with triumph, Vince gave a little shake and took himself over to Dad.

'You're a very brave lad, Vince,' Dad told him.' I wouldn't lie there if you paid me!'

Dad took hold of the reins and we all walked home.

'Lots of jobs still to do, sorry, Tamsin. Once you've put Oscar away, I need help to reset the wind turbine and Mum needs a hand to pump water up.' I grimaced. By the time I'd primed our wind turbine – which actually meant winding it up – and pumped up the water, I would feel as if I'd built up enough heat to shower all of us including Vince and Oscar (who both hated showers as much as I did then.) 'I know, it's a pain, but if you want a shower . . . and you definitely need one . . . !' And then he started to run for it.

Home was built round a large cave in the side of an east-facing ridge that had spectacular views over the river and valley beyond. In the distance, on a clear day, we could see a tiny church over twenty miles away, set upon its own tor, marking the edge of Edgecombe Moor.

We called it our 'Eco Pad'. A house and animal barn combined, like the long houses people built centuries ago; but there the similarities ended. From its grass roof studded with photovoltaic cells to its geothermal heating it was green and carbon neutral.

It was also invisible until you got within fifty metres of the house door.

Which is where we were when all hell broke loose.

I was starting to imagine the fragrant lamb casserole in the oven, made from our own meat and vegetables, when there was a terrific roar overhead and, out of nowhere, a helicopter materialised.

Several things happened in quick succession. Dad dragged me off Oscar and told me to drop to the ground. As my feet touched the ground he'd got the girth unstrapped and was pulling off the saddle. I started to help with the bridle but he shouted at me.

'Drop, Tamsin! For once *do* as you're asked, *when* you're asked! Wriggle and get under the hedge!'

Surprised at his voice, rough and impatient, so unlike himself, I wriggled as he said, hardly noticing Mum's far from gentle hands hauling me under the cover of the hedge. Where had she come from? Once there, she let go, but I felt her shaking. I watched open-mouthed as Dad slapped Oscar's large rump and then dived into some bracken edging the field!

What on earth was going on, I couldn't guess. Oscar was clearly frightened of the helicopter and hadn't really needed the slap of encouragement to make him bolt to the farthest side of the big field to try to escape from the deafening roar. Had Dad known he'd be terrified and dragged me off to prevent an accident? Why then had he dived under the bracken?

The helicopter circled and circled. I'd never seen one so close before. Mum's shaking continued. The noise was overpowering. We couldn't speak. I longed to hug her but we stayed where we were until the helicopter had flown away.

Only then did Dad emerge from his hiding place, bits of bracken sticking out from all over him. He came and hugged us, then we all trooped in, washed our hands and had our lovely meal, as if nothing had happened!

Well I wasn't going to let it rest there! What did they think I was – a baby? Did they think I hadn't noticed anything? Of course I'd seen helicopters before, but in the distance. We'd seen them as we'd been out and about in our fields, on the moor. We'd carried on as normal. We'd heard them from inside the Pad, but that hadn't seemed to worry Mum and Dad like this. Well, I would ask them later on, when we'd settled down after supper.

I always loved that time after supper. All the jobs done, cosy and warm with the thick 'black-out' curtains closed. I was home schooled then and this was when the big globe came out and we'd work out how many hours of sunlight people in places like Norway and South Africa would be getting, using balls of wool for the sun and moon. It was when I did my maths and read books about explorers and scientists and their dis-coveries. We played CDs and DVDs and on an old fashioned video player watched films, which gave me a good idea of life in the cities: totally different from our life in Cornwall. Much though it interested and informed me, I knew where I preferred to live, forever! Dad said we didn't get any 'reception' where we were, so that ruled out televisions, computers and mobile phones.

Fine by me. On that day, I had everything I could possibly need. Except a trick riding saddle of course, and that was promised for the next day.

I even went to bed early, so that the next day would come more quickly. I'd completely forgotten about the helicopter. But I was so excited I couldn't get to sleep and then I remembered it! I would ask them now. So I got out of bed and headed to the family room where I could hear them talking.

Then I stopped, shocked. Mum and Dad *were* talking – to another person in the room!

We never had visitors! I barged in.

'Who's here?' I asked.

The voices and light snapped off. The silence was so dense that it felt like a wall, pushing me back. I hesitated for a second, unsure.

Dad spoke. But it didn't really sound like him. This voice was brittle, edgy.

'Er. Hi there honey, there's no one here, just Mum and I talking. Hurry on back to bed, before you get cold.' But while all this seemed reasonable, I could hear scuffling and Mum still hadn't spoken.

I'd never been brushed off like this before so I ignored the instruction, turned on the light and walked right in.

Kneeling on the floor, my parents were throwing things into a large metal box I didn't recognise. It had obviously come from a cupboard by the fire where a small door in the wall was open. I hadn't even known about the cupboard. Usually there was a large picture of a badger hanging there.

'What's that?' I asked. They hadn't stopped putting whatever it was, away.

'It's a radio, love,' said Mum.

So? It was no big deal. I knew what a radio was. Why all the secrecy?

'I thought we didn't have good enough reception,' I started.

'Well we do,' said Dad, 'it's just been a simpler way of explaining it.'

'Explaining what?' I persisted.

'Explaining that every night we need to get in touch with the Underground Resistance. Secretly. Without our daughter knowing.'

This was no good. None of it made sense.

'Tamsin honey, we need to start from the beginning,' Dad began, but Mum groaned. 'Oh not yet, please. Surely she's too young.'

I rolled onto the rug and put my arms round Vince. Could he understand any of this?

'This all started long before you were born,' Dad kicked off, 'when a very tiny part of the world was full of people who had far too much. The larger part was full of people who did not have enough to eat or to live on. In addition the whole world was very advanced technically, especially the tiny part. It had grown very complicated and entirely dependent on computer technology to run everything. Lots of the old traditional skills were lost and oil was the major energy source.'

'Here in the United Kingdom there was a coup and a group of people took control away from the people and the government,' continued Mum. 'This group, or regime, took over the UK Internet and all the communication satellite systems, just long enough to establish itself. That's what your dad means about depending on computer technology. Everything was taken out at once and no-one could fix it in time.'

'It was called a 'bloodless' coup,' said Dad. But we were a monarchy then and the king and queen and their children were killed, as well as most of their relatives and people who worked for them. They didn't seem to count in the statistics.' He paused and swallowed. After a few seconds Mum continued.

'In the first few years it was about consolidating control. Then everybody had to register to receive things like food, water, energy, communications, access to health and education. But we soon found out that they were adding drugs to our water so they could control us too.'

'What sort of drugs?' I asked. I could hardly take this in. How could all this have been happening around me, and I hadn't noticed?

'Tranquillisers to calm us down, so we wouldn't make trouble. Soon people were addicted and walking round like zombies. Then things called contraceptives that stopped women having babies. But people aren't stupid. They soon recognised what was happening. And when they did, they started to rebel and publicise it. They were known as dissidents and from then on they started to be hunted down by the regime.'

'Hunted? Like fox hunting?' It was the only hunting I knew. I had just been allowed to ride in the junior section of the weekly local hunt, to start that September.

'Worse. Far worse,' Mum was emphatic. 'They went on the hunt for people with information and knowledge because they were the ones they feared most. Scientists like your dad and me: teachers, doctors and intellectuals: artists, writers and musicians – people who could influence others. They hunted them down, tortured them and when the prisons were full, killed them.'

'How did you get away? Was I born?' I asked, curious and frightened in equal parts.

'We weren't supposed to have a baby without permission. So when we knew I was pregnant we ran away as far as we could, to the very edge of the country here in Cornwall. And we became farmers.' She nodded at Dad, who said,

'It was tough at first but it became easier to hide as time went on. Because of the controls on oil, people in the country went back to using horses, so no vehicles were being taxed. Tens of thousands of people like us took refuge in the country and births, deaths and marriages stopped being registered by computer almost immediately. So it became virtually impossible to track people down in rural areas. And once we'd changed our name . . .'

I couldn't contain myself any longer.

'Changed our name? To what?'

'To Farmer,' Dad said.

'So I am not Tamsin Farmer?' I shouted. 'You don't even trust *me* with the truth?'

I felt so angry and hurt, not to mention scared. My universe had disintegrated. I reacted the only way I knew at that age. I stormed to my room and flung myself on my bed, crying so much that my head hurt.

No one came after me, not even Vince. So, once I'd calmed down I went back to sit on the cushions between my parents. Vince crawled up carefully. 'Why couldn't you trust me?' I whispered. 'I'd never give you away.'

'We can't even trust *ourselves* to tell the truth, honey,' Dad said sadly. 'They have truth drugs that make you tell everything you know. *You* can never betray *us* because you don't know our real names. On the other hand, your mum and I know too much and would betray each other and even you. That's why we must never ever be caught.'

'We registered your birth in a tiny church, like they used to centuries ago. No one will find it,' Mum told me. 'As far as these evil people are concerned, Tamsin doesn't exist. If you are caught they cannot link you with anyone else. There are millions outside their net, scratching livings, trying to keep the old knowledge.'

'We've got most of the technology,' Dad butted in, 'the photovoltaics and the wind turbines for example and we're learning how we can keep these in good repair. So we can power radios like this, and computers and all sorts of things. And as long as we don't use satellites, which can be monitored, we can use the technology and we can communicate with each other.'

'Who are we? Is this the, the Underground . . .' I was back to the questions again.

'Resistance. We call it the 'Tube' for short,' Mum smiled.

'Why?' I asked innocently. They exploded.

'Never mind,' laughed Dad, 'it's too complicated.'

For that read, can't be bothered to explain, you're probably too young to understand anyway. I hated it when they did this, so I sulked quietly into Vince's neck while they controlled themselves.

Dad now pulled a wooden box out of the metal one. It had knobs and dials on it. Then three pairs of headphones.

'This is an old fashioned radio which was used for communication, before even the first satellites had been launched.'

The radio was a wind up one with a large red knob on one corner. He switched on, then depressed the red knob which sounded as a series of long and short beeps.

'That's called Morse code,' he said. 'It's a signal that calls a listener up. Here, put these on.' He handed me the headphones. 'Now listen carefully.'

There were squeaks and groans and high pitched scratching noises before it all went clear and a voice in my ears said,

'This is Vince's brother, Vince's brother calling Vince. Can you hear me Vince?'

'Vince's brother?' I squealed, 'Who's Vince's brother? Who knows about Vince?'

Vince's brother said urgently, 'Confirm you are there Vince or I will close down in three, two . . .'

'It's OK Vince's brother,' laughed Dad, 'it is Vince here. But Vince's daughter has found you out.'

Vince's daughter? I glanced at Vince lying amongst all the cables and knobs and dials. He looked as though he'd lost the plot. Just like me.

'Vince hasn't got a daughter,' I said primly, 'he's had an operation!'

The radio suddenly developed a fit of the cackles of its own which took a few seconds to subside.

'Vince's daughter sounds just like Vince's wife,' Vince's brother spluttered, 'all very proper!'

'If I am Vince's daughter who are you?' I glared at Dad, wanting to be in on the joke.

'I'm your uncle.'

My small world had just doubled in size.

'I didn't know I had any relatives. Wow! Have I ever seen you?'

'The last time I met you, I think you were in a cot and used to go to sleep when you were put to bed.'

'What are you . . . where are you . . . Uncle . . . Vince's brother?'

'Certain questions not allowed, Vince's daughter! Ask Vince, when we're finished. Now, are there any more questions that I can answer for you?'

'Did you do jousting and things?' I was watching Mum's face as I asked. It was non-committal.

'No, not me. Ask Vince's wife. She always knitted a lot of chainmail as far as I can remember. She'll fill you in. Great to talk to you. Speak soon. Goodbye now. Keep safe.'

I took off the headphones. Dad and my newly discovered uncle continued with their conversation. Mum and I went to my room, arm in arm.

'What does the Tube do, Mum,' I asked thoughtfully.

'It's fighting to restore a rightful, elected government,' she said. 'It will take a long time and a lot of brave lives. But we will do it.'

'Mum, I'll never give you away, I promise I won't.'

'I know you'll try with all your might, my love.'

Now although we still went to the St Peter's Fair next day and I got my trick riding saddle, nothing was the same again. The games we played were really lessons in survival. Our green existence was actually about concealment. Our social isolation was not from choice. It was about security. The helicopters were Spy Birds and were our deadly hunters.

That was the day I grew up.

It was the day I entered the warzone.

# CHAPTER 1

*Two Years Later*

I smelt the smoke as soon as we rounded White Stone Head. Sliding down from the saddle, I pushed Oscar back into the under hang of the White Stone and dropped his reins to the ground. He'd stay put until I told him. Crawling back I reached the lookout point and clamped the anti-reflective binoculars to my eyes. The approach had been chosen for this very purpose – maximum view of our house, from maximum distance away.

Feeling sick I focused. I could almost guess what I was going to see.

Dad never lit bonfires. If you want to advertise your position to anyone, he said, light a bonfire. Even from space, you can see a big bonfire. And this was a big one.

In the back of my consciousness I could hear a SpyBird. Like a goshawk, always on the lookout, always hunting . . .

With a jump I remembered the drill and scrambled under the cover of a gorse bush and looked again. The sight made me sob out aloud.

Dad and Mum had purposely designed our house so that it could not be seen from above. Normally invisible from more than fifty metres away because of its rough grass roof, it now showed its belly to the world. The roof had almost burnt out. The frame beneath, constructed from stout branches and half tree trunks, was burning so well the flames were shooting metres up into the air.

But where were Mum and Dad? This morning, when I had gone to look at our sheep and cows with Oscar, I had left them doing the usual jobs for a sunny summer's day. Dad had kept Vince to help him at home.

I scanned the whole site. No movement. Were they inside? I screamed out – 'NO!' They must have been able to get out. It was a single storey building, with doors front back and side. So why weren't they trying to put out the fire? There was plenty of water – the water butts, the borehole . . . where were they?

By now my sub consciousness had caught up

– the SpyBird was moving away, not closer, so it was safe to come out of my scratchy hiding hole.

Still no movement.

I was bursting to rush home, but we had rules. The Rules – our homely compendium of tips for sticky situations that you might come upon in your everyday life. And our everyday life? Well, not the carefree mix of animals, riding and learning which I'd believed as a child. Now I knew it to be a chilling game of avoiding the agents and spies coming from London, combined with coaxing a living from difficult moorland soil. The Rules – drummed into me by my security-obsessed parents. If you come upon an incident, wait five minutes. Often the enemy will move within five minutes. Mostly your brain cools down as well.

Five minutes. Seemed like an eternity. But I was fifteen minutes' ride away and five more minutes wasn't going to make a scrap of difference. To anyone. In that bonfire.

So I spent it crying. Seemed a good way – pouring it out. The only family, friends, home I had – all gone up in flames. They deserved more than five minutes, but I had to get down there, find out what had happened, if I could do anything.

Oscar wasn't keen on going into a smoke cloud

but years of partnership gave him enough trust to take us in. At about fifteen metres it became too much so I jumped off, dropped the reins and covered the rest on foot.

The front of the house was now just a heap of ash and glowing rafters, so the fire must have been burning for about two hours. Dad had told me that the green oak that had been used would take about this long to burn through. There was no access from the front, but what about the back?

The house had been built around a natural stone archway, which led into a dark granite cave where the animals were housed in the winter. Thank goodness it was summer. Our three jersey cows and little flock of Jacob sheep were safe and sound on the common moor. That was where I had been all morning. But maybe the barn end would burn slower and I could get into the house from there?

As soon as I went through the stone arch I knew that my mission was impossible. The flames from the house were raging so hot and high that even if Mum and Dad were in there, they would have been well and truly incinerated by now.

For some reason I yelled. I yelled with desperation. I yelled with anguish. I yelled with the unfairness and hopelessness of it all.

Suddenly, there was a howl. A tiny, thready,

high-pitched howl penetrating the deafening roar of the flames.

Vince. What was he doing here? While these thoughts were tumbling about I ripped off my top and ran outside and dropped it in the drinking trough. I draped it over my head and shoulders and went in yelling again – '*Vince! Vince!*'

The smoke was suffocating but I knew where he should be – inside Oscar's stall in the barn. That's where he liked to sleep. But why wouldn't he come to me?

The reason almost made me throw up. He had been tied up. To the ring where we normally tied the horse. Vince never got tied up.

Someone had tied him up – then left him to die slowly and horribly. Had they done the same with my parents?

Actually it was easy to release him; the rope was charred all the way through. But he was on fire and we only had seconds left. I tore off my wet top and threw it over his burning coat, then picked him up and ran, both of us screaming and yelping until we were in the trough and the ice cold water had dowsed the flames and cooled down our burns. Vince's feet were the worst affected, his thick fur had protected the rest of him. My chest had been scorched in a couple of places when I'd lifted him up, but my wet top had done the trick and protected me. We'd survive, and we had each other. I nuzzled his neck, smelling the bitter, charred smell of burnt fur.

And touched something unexpected.

I jerked back my head to see what it was. Instead of the leather collar I was expecting, my nose had touched a neckerchief. Someone had tied a neckerchief around his neck. Not only that, it was the red one. The Rules said – Red for danger. Red for RUN. NOW! My heart leapt. Despite the extreme danger I now found myself in, this meant only one thing. My parents had managed to leave a message. They could still be alive!

Suddenly aware of my surroundings again, I swivelled my head around. Someone could be watching me. This creepy thought made me shiver. All thoughts of self-pity and smarting burns evaporated as I hauled myself and a very heavy, waterlogged Vince, out of the trough. While he had a good shake I whistled up Oscar. Vince would have to travel aboard with me until I could do something about his pads.

Slinging him onto the saddle I told him to stay and dropped the reins again. There was one last thing I must try to do.

# CHAPTER 2

Looking at the embers of the huge bonfire, which was all that remained of our
house, it was difficult to work out where
our family room had been. The big structural rafters that Dad had hewn out of living oak were
still partially there but had collapsed. I was looking for where the radio was kept. If nothing had
happened to it since this morning, it should still
be in its fireproof steel box. If I could rescue it,
there was a chance I could contact someone in
the Underground Resistance (or 'Tube' for short.
Mum had eventually explained it to me, as I'd
never been to London.) They might know what
had happened here today.

I soon began to regret it. It seemed a hopeless
task. The ash was far too hot to wade through.
Picking up a few stones I threw them at likely
looking mounds with no success. The minutes

were ticking and with each one it was becoming more dangerous to remain. In frustration I slung the last stone in with all my strength. It went 'clunk'.

Slap in the middle, but having found it I wasn't going to leave it. Grabbing a bucket I filled it from the trough and threw it over the still glowing ashes. The idea was to cool down a trail to the radio, run along it and carry it back. It wasn't very heavy.

Bad idea. Clouds of steam and ashes erupted from the first bucketful. Still far too hot. I needed a huge quantity of water to flow over the target. Where would there be such a large amount? Think, brain.

The water butts had burnt. Trying not to panic and ever more conscious of those who could be watching and even now closing in, I remembered.

The backup tank. Above roof level, in the bank at the rear of the barn, it was fed from a natural spring. It was there to fill the water butts in times of drought, which in Cornwall was rare. The last one had been nine years ago.

That should work. If I could get the brass tap open.

I scrambled up the bank, thinking that after nine years it would probably be seized up.

It was. However, a couple of hard hits with a

lump of granite did the trick. The slate lined tank slowly emptied itself down the bank and through the ash field that had been our house, forming a hissing, black track as it snaked on down the slope.

I slid back down and followed the sludgy path in. So pleased with myself that the plan had worked I completely forgot that the box would be burning hot and for the second time in an hour was plunging my hands into the water trough, swearing at my stupidity.

While soaking, I looked around for a tool to help and noticed the mucking out fork lying where I'd left it that morning. For once my untidiness had paid off and with the fork I managed to push the box completely out of the ashes and tip it over on the cool grass. It had no lock and the radio fell out, hot but intact.

A quick glance at my solar watch showed that an hour had passed since I'd seen the RUN NOW message. Not exactly a text book response Tamsin Farmer. Try harder next time.

Gathering all the radio components together I stuffed them into a saddlebag, swung into the saddle around Vince who was fast asleep and headed for my hideout. Aware of possible observers I would have to use the longest, most indirect, approach. I would need to be constantly on the lookout for an ambush. Looking at the comatose Vince, I felt I was missing my right hand man.

Mum, Dad and I each had our own secret hideout. This was so that if we ever got caught we couldn't give the others away, even under truth drugs. When I was small I used to share Mum's but for the last two years I'd had my own. I'd changed it three times since then. Like playing hide and seek when you're little, you think you're invisible just because you can't see round a tree, while everyone else can see your arms and legs sticking out. So mine had got better each time. It held emergency rations, cash, some clothes and basic camping gear.

The approach was extremely important. Convoluted, hidden, but most of all giving the best view over your surroundings. You had to be sure you were unobserved before you finally committed.

My choice that afternoon was by Gallows Tor. For much of the way it used the highest path. Having climbed all the way to the top I knew that no one could look down on me and I felt more secure. All right, we could be a little exposed here, above the tree line, but at this time of the summer the bracken gave a lot of cover.

With one last binocular sweep of the lower valley it was all clear and we quickly dropped the few metres into the shelter of the woodland fringe.

Quietly we waited at the edge of the hideout clearing. There was no sound.

Something wasn't quite right but I couldn't put my finger on it. Vince lay still, snoring quietly. Oscar's ears were relaxed. I needed the food and other things hidden in my little cave. I slid off.

As soon as my feet touched the ground I knew what was wrong.

There was no sound.

But it was too late. Now there was too much sound – as the crunch of his feet on the under carpet of dried leaves gave my stalker away. And then his big muscular forearm was around my shoulder and throat immobilising me in a stifling grip. He smelled of sweat and unwashed clothes. His breath stank.

'Pretty good for a young 'un,' he rasped, 'just not quite good enough for me!'

# CHAPTER 3

He was pushing me to the ground, following me down, giving me no room for manoeuvre. A rope was ready in one hand and soon I would be trussed up and helpless.

'How did you find me?' I mumbled, trying not to taste the soil in my teeth. I needed time. I needed some room.

'Oh, you were good. I was down here. I just caught you by chance on the top up there. Was your horse that did it. Sun caught on his white bits. You've done this before, 'aven't you? Practised?'

No comment. But he hadn't followed me from home. That might mean this was a random event.

He had the rope round my wrists now. I had to distract him. This was my last chance. I needed a diversion, something to give me a fraction of space.

I took a deep breath. 'He. .lp!' I cried in a pathetic high-pitched voice. More like a whistle really. Or so I hoped.

He laughed. 'There's no one to hear you, laddie, never mind help you. .'

Wrong. Because here came the sound of pounding hooves, then a whinny. I couldn't see but guessed Oscar was trying a rear and stand. Help had arrived then.

The man coughed. Once. As though the air had been punched from his lungs. And if he'd mistaken my gender, I forgave him.

His grip loosened a fraction. Enough for me to break my hands out of his grip. But then his whole weight disappeared from my back altogether and I rolled over and out of his way.

His problem was a large ferocious attacking fur ball whose razor teeth were slashing his back and neck. In his efforts to protect himself he had completely forgotten me. Jumping up, I balanced, then aimed a kick at his undefended solar plexus. He crumpled, unconscious.

First time I'd tried that kick in anger. Very pleased with the result.

Vince painfully limped over and sniffed the body before coming over to me for a tummy rub. Oscar had his head down at a clump of tender grasses.

'Nice when a plan comes together, eh?' I whispered. I looked at my attacker. His clothes were filthy and worn and he had long straggly grey hair and a rough beard. Was he just a thief who'd found a victim?

Suddenly there was a strange buzzing noise. It seemed to be coming from him. Vince looked intently at one of his pockets. I felt inside and picked out a small rectangular device with a tiny flashing screen.

A mobile phone? I'd never actually seen one before but Dad had told me about them. They were off limits to those of us trying to live undetected lives. If it was a phone, it meant that it could be located by satellite. It also meant he wasn't alone. We'd better be gone.

Quickly I tied the man up with his own rope and gagged him with his neckerchief. Having no idea how to disable it I smashed the device against a tree and threw the scrambled mess high up into the branches. That should pose a few problems for anyone trying to locate it.

This time I ran into my hideout unhindered and stuffed the emergency rations and clothes into the other saddlebag. With Vince loaded once more and all signs of the struggle covered with leaves we quickly left and descended deep into the woods.

To my second hideout.

'Always have a backup backup.' Mum's words seemed to ring in my ears when half an hour later we reached the very centre of the plantation.

I had been riding in here ever since the pines and larches had been spindly saplings and light was abundant. Now they were big strong trees with a dark impenetrable canopy. The advantage was that Oscar and I knew our way around very well. Anyone new to the territory would struggle.

It was really dark in here now, made even gloomier by the high earth banks that had been created to provide shelter to the young saplings when first planted. Families of badgers had built setts in the banks and I'd enjoyed watching their antics from behind the bivouac that I'd plaited from creepers and leaves. It had taken almost a year to complete. It wasn't waterproof, like my cave, but all three of us could hide behind this curtain and be completely invisible.

Once inside, it was time to tackle the radio. It could be powered either by clockwork or solar. No choice in these dark surroundings so I started to crank it up with its built in handle. About sixty turns for fifteen minutes' worth of electricity.

Eyes closed, winding, I remembered that time when I was twelve, seeing this radio for the first time. I thought communication meant talking, shouting or whistling to my parents and animals. From that night I learnt about the Internet and computers and it was wonderful and exciting. But out of bounds for us, because anything with a microchip could become the means of finding us.

It had been exciting. But it was a two-edged sword because alongside it came the knowledge of the danger, which stalked our lives daily.

There was a high-pitched whine and I hastily plugged the earphones into the socket. Carefully I turned the tuner knob until I could hear the clear tone of transmission mode. This type of radio, often called the 'ham' radio in old times, was the only one that could not be located by satellite. It made it the only form of distance communication that Tube members could use. If they were careful. But conversations could be listened into and there were thousands of people whose job it was to eavesdrop for the regime and so the conversations had to be in code.

Since that first night my uncle and I had become very good friends and it was him I was trying to contact. I transmitted his call sign using the red knob.

The radio crackled and whished into life.

'This is Vince's brother! Who's calling?'

I was so pleased to hear him I burst into tears. Must have made a terrible noise his end.

'It's Vince's daughter!'

'Thank goodness!'

'I need to see a dentist.'(HELP!)

'How's the tooth?' (WHAT'S WRONG?)

'I've lost Vince. He vanished. Like a . . . a bird,' I said lamely. I was now convinced that the Spy-Bird had not been there by coincidence. It must have taken them away. But where to?

'Yes, I know. At the moment he's completely lost. I'm working on it. Where are you? Careful now.' That was a warning not to give anything away.

'Counting' (TO A HUNDRED, HIDE AND SEEK, HIDING) 'but Vince . . .' Here I faltered. I was on the verge of tears again. I could hear Vince in the darkness, licking and licking his painful paws. He desperately needed help. I would have to risk it.

I gabbled 'Vince's pet has burnt his feet and I've no ointment.'

'Oh dear. All right. For all these things you need to go and see a specialist. I'll give you his number. Got a pencil?'

At the ready. A notebook too. I took down the number risking a flick of the torch to do it. It was a standard telephone number. You ignore the first three digits and the last eight digits give you the map coordinates. I'd look those up in a minute. The instructions were still coming. How my uncle had arranged all this so quickly was a mystery to me but it should have been very comforting that he had.

Except that despite all the whistles and crackles, I was becoming convinced that this was not Vince's brother I was speaking to. What should I do?

'You need to look for the round tablers,' the man said then.

'Repeat please.' Even if this was the enemy, the only thing this conversation revealed was that I was still alive. And they knew that anyway. I concentrated.

'When you find the round tablers tomorrow, you must stay with them for a while. Is Oscar with you?'

'Yes.'

'Good. You'll need him. Ready to sign off?'

'Affirmative.'

'Try not to worry. Leave everything to me. Delilah sends her love.'

The battery light was fading. We said our goodbyes and switched off. I flopped onto the soft earth floor of the hide. I was exhausted.

The carefully coded message was very clear. Go and stay with the 'round tablers', whoever they were and stay put. In other words, don't try and find your parents yourself.

So I was on my own then.

It did answer one question though. The man I'd been talking to was a Tube member. He'd used Delilah, the correct code word.

But that opened up a bigger question.

What on earth had happened to Vince's brother, my uncle?

# CHAPTER 4

First things first. I got the map out and spread it over Oscar who had lain down on the cool earth. With my torch on its lowest setting I found the co-ordinates. Birkhampton.

I went over our strange conversation. I was to go to Birkhampton and meet up with some round tablers tomorrow where I would be able to stay. And I would need Oscar. Well of course I would need Oscar! It was about twenty miles away! While I had the map out I quickly plotted my route there. We would travel overnight and keep to the back lanes and bridle paths. By the time it got light we should be very close to Birkhampton and we could find somewhere sheltered to have a sleep. We'd rest and continue on the road later in the morning when there should be plenty of other people about. Hopefully by then I would have worked out what 'round tablers' were.

I should take my first bearing now, while there was a little light. When we started off it would be pitch black and everything would be a lot more difficult. So I peeked out of the shelter and took it – a tree with a distinctive branch, which from this angle looked like a long nose. Then I fished out the emergency rations – biscuits that Mum and I had baked a few weeks before, still good in the air-tight tin. Dried apples and blackcurrants from our orchard, too. Eating them made me realise that our simple way of life, linked into the rhythms of the seasons, was all over. What might the future be like?

I chucked some of the biscuits to Vince and got back to the business of surviving the next twenty-four hours. I'd never rescue anyone if I kept on blubbering!

'Round tablers'. Some sort of carpenters who made round tables? A café where they had round tables . . . ?

Fragments of dreams inhabited my restless sleep. Me, snatching up the red neckerchief from Vince's collar, swung low on Oscar's flank. Mum, laughing, knitting metres and metres of chainmail so I could be a 'real' knight. Then we were under the stars and Mum was teaching me how to take bearings and navigate by them. Then she was laughing and we were all counting and playing hide and seek in the dark.

The dreams were all happy. Which made the sickening sense of loss each time I woke even worse. All I wanted was to escape back into that dream world. When my watch alarm buzzed at two I was shattered.

But I had now solved the riddle of the round tablers. Well, my dreams had, full as they had been with knights. The Knights of the *Round Table*. Of course! Now all I had to do was to find some knights. In Birkhampton. Didn't seem likely.

'Hope you slept better than I did,' I whispered to Oscar as I pulled his girth up, 'we've got about twenty miles to do before the next stop.' He grunted, but I think that was the girth. I led him out from behind the bivouac, carefully lifted Vince onto the sheepskin saddle cover and followed him up.

It was almost pitch black in the heart of the woods. If anyone was waiting for me surely they'd have given up by now? I could emerge from any one of an infinite number of points. Providing I was careful, the darkness would be my friend.

Switching on the infrared of my binoculars I picked out the tree I'd taken my first bearing from. Fox and hounds in the dark. I'd played this game lots of times. But it took on a sinister edge knowing there could be a real pack in pursuit. There were plenty of animals caught up in my regular binocular sweeps – deer grazing, foxes on their business, badgers housekeeping, but instead of my heart jumping for joy as it usually did on these sorts of expeditions, it leapt with alarm at every new movement.

I was glad when we broke free of the plantation and suddenly I could see unaided again. It was cloudy but with plenty of breaks so that the moonlight flickered through. Perfect for our needs. Just enough light to find our way, not enough to throw us into silhouette. We headed east.

I knew the way to Birkhampton well enough, by daylight that is. Every year we took honey, eggs and wool to the agricultural show. We took the trap and always had a night under canvas on Endecombe Moor on the way back. It was our summer holiday.

Worried I might lose my way in the dark, I was glad of the moon's help and soon was spotting familiar landmarks, like the derelict wooden chapel and a distinctive symmetrical conical hill, bare except for a stand of silver birches on the top.

It was good to have a purpose at last! But as we briskly walked and trotted on along the green lanes and bridle paths questions arose. What was I going to do when I got to Birkhampton? How was that going to lead me to Mum and Dad?

My mind drifted to conversations I'd had with them since my 'Enlightenment'. At first, I'd been fascinated by the story of how we had all escaped from the cruel dictators who had taken over. How the old king and queen had been killed and how it was believed the new king, queen and small daughter had gone into hiding abroad,

Later, though, I'd wanted to know why it had happened. How could a democratic country just be taken over like that? By its own people?

'Because of apathy and indifference,' Dad had said. 'Every election the same people won. Every election less people voted because they thought it wasn't worth the effort. Eventually one group of people controlled parliament. The same people in power, decade after decade.'

'But that shouldn't have mattered as long as they were doing a good job?' I'd been puzzled.

'Agreed. But they became corrupted by the power and they had no opposition. And they didn't want their rule to end. They had cleverly appointed the heads of the military into govern-ment without most people noticing or caring. Then they mounted a coup. They closed down the Internet into and out of the United King-dom, shut down all mobile phones and closed all the main television and radio stations. It only took a week. Most people were unaware of what was going on. But once communications were switched on again it was a different story. Naturally many people objected. They didn't want to live in a dictatorship. And very soon the killings began. And the abductions, and torture and truth drugs.'

My reverie was shattered by voices. We had reached a little footbridge that crossed over a huge road, a dual carriageway. It used to carry all the traffic in and out of the county. Overgrown and reclaimed by wild grasses, it was still used as a thoroughfare, but now for foot and horse transport.

Focusing with the binoculars, at first I could only see the grass tracks going in each direction. Then I saw them. A group of four, walking towards the bridge I was standing on. All were dressed the same and with their steps matching so closely it looked like they were marching. Except for one at the back who was much slighter and nowhere near as tall as the rest and who was marching double time to keep up. Were they soldiers? And if so, what were they doing, here, at this time of night?

I didn't want to find out! Squeezing Oscar on I flattened myself over Vince and we quietly walked over to the other side, looking, I hoped, like nothing more than a stray animal crossing.

The dawn sky was streaked with pale primrose as we reached Moorton Cross. I needed to find shelter before the sun came up. A half derelict stone barn in the top corner of a field adjoining the moor looked ideal.

Vince limped painfully to a chattering moorland stream, drank deeply then flopped down in it, cooling his sore paws. Oscar drank and would have had a roll if I had let him. Silly horse still had his saddle on! With my water bottle full I led them up the hill to the barn. Inside were some dusty old straw bales. Once these were teased apart they made a comfortable bed for Vince and me. With Oscar tethered out of sight of the track, we were on our bed when the sun blazed out through the charcoal clouds minutes later. This time my sleep was dreamless.

. . . .

'There is someone here! I told you there was! Mum!'

I was torn from my peaceful slumber it seemed like only seconds later, by the high pitched yelling of a child. This shocking voice was followed round the corner of the barn wall by its owner, a small boy in shorts and shirt with an untidy head of red hair. Another, smaller redhead followed more cautiously and then became a whole, even smaller girl. Having found me, they then stood and stared silently until help arrived, in the form of their mother. Well, I guessed so, as she also had the red hair. By now, I knew there was no means of escape, if I needed it. I was hoping that this was an innocent encounter but you couldn't guarantee anything and where the heck had Vince got to? He hadn't warned me – surely he wasn't going to do the heroic thing again like yesterday against the robber? But no, because here he was in the arms of a big, black-bearded man, the fourth member of the group to turn up in my makeshift bedroom.

'Is 'e yours?' he asked. A man of few words and unsmiling face, but he had kind blue eyes and he was cradling Vince in a gentle way. Vince was attempting to lick his face. We were lost.

' 'is feet are very sore,' the man added, 'ave you got somethin' for 'im?'

'No, I haven't,' I replied. To be honest, I was very worried. My little first aid kit had nothing for problems on this scale. 'We had an accident and I haven't been able to . . .'

He put up his hand to stop me. 'Looks like 'es been burnt, poor feller. I might 'ave summat on the wagon' and he turned, still carrying Vince, and strolled out of sight.

Everyone else had been silent during all this but as soon as the dark man had disappeared all the noise started again. I got up and stretched and tried to discreetly pack my stuff away.

'Actually our horse sensed yours,' said the mother apologetically. 'She gave a little whinny, yours called back and then the children wanted to come and see what a horse was doing in a ruined barn. Sorry to spoil your nap!'

And all this while I was asleep. I was easy prey.

'It must be time I was up anyway,' I said. Glancing at my watch it confirmed this and then my stomach gave an enormous gurgle. When I would eat next was anybody's guess. My rations were all gone. The children giggled.

'Where are you all going?' I asked, trying to divert attention from the rumbling.

'Oh, we're just having a half day off. It was such a lovely day it seemed a shame to be working all the time.' She spoke without an accent, unlike her husband.

'And we've brought a picnic,' whispered the little girl shyly, her arm securely round her mother's leg.

'Shall we have it here? Would you like some?' demanded the boy.

'Good idea!' agreed their parent. 'Go and tell your dad, and we can bring Josie and the wagon up the track. Oh. If that's all right with you?' she asked, with a laugh. 'Sorry, I took it for granted!'

Of course it was all right! The boy ran off and soon the man drove up the short track with Vince on the front bench, already looking much more comfortable. He'd had comfrey, witch hazel and chickweed rubbed in and then been bandaged with clean strips of cloth. I was even given the remainder of the ointment to take with us.

'Are you always so well prepared?' I asked, curiously, but we were busy tethering the horses so they could drink from the stream and the man didn't answer.

The family shared an enormous picnic of egg sandwiches, (from their own chickens the little girl confided), apple cake that the children had helped their mother to make and their own blackcurrant cordial. A real country picnic from a self-sufficient family like ours was – or had been, I thought with a sudden piercing sadness.

The time came too soon when I would have to leave. I still had no idea where I should head for once I got to Birkhampton – all I knew was that some knights possibly might be there. I was tempted to ask the couple, they must surely be local, but it would be too dangerous to let anyone know my intentions.

Anyway, I had already stayed too long. I was

starting to get the feeling that our meeting wasn't entirely unplanned. Finding me, having the ointment, the picnic – it all seemed a bit coincidental. And now the couple were giving each other looks, and the hairs on the back of my neck were beginning to stand on end.

I started tacking up Oscar, preparing for flight.

The man cleared his throat. 'Erm, would it mean anything to you if I said Delilah?' Suddenly his accent had disappeared, too.

I jumped. There was no way, at that moment, that I could have hidden my surprise but I tried to stay calm.

'How do you know that?' I gasped.

The man smiled now, relieved. 'We were told a young person with a horse and a dog with damaged feet. It was fortunate our horse Josie found you, but we would have carried on looking all day if she hadn't. We came to help – and now we must go. There's a message. Ron.'

'Ron?' I repeated. 'What does that mean?'

'I'm afraid we don't know – and we don't want to,' the woman said, gently pressing her fingers to my lips. 'The less we know, the less we can tell.' She was still kind, but an urgency had set in. Now they knew I was the right one, the longer they were with me the more dangerous it was for them.

The woman gave me a farewell hug. She was like my mum – brave and kind – all the more reason that I should keep going. The children just thought it had been a big adventure. I'd been like that, learning all the woodcraft and the tracking. It was all fun when you were little. I hoped they would never lose their brave parents . . .

We set off in opposite directions, waving our farewells until we were out of sight. Then the three of us set our faces towards Birkhampton and the next steps on our journey to get Mum and Dad back.

# CHAPTER 5

We were on a path that followed an old railway line, pulled up in the old times and transformed into a bridle path and cycle trail. It was a direct route into Birkhampton and safe for travellers like me because it avoided the surveillance points. These were on the big main routes like the old dual carriageway I had crossed over earlier. The line on this stretch had been built on an embankment so the track was above the line of the hedges, heavy now with the fruit of wild brambles. This gave me a good all round view of the landscape while the overgrown hedges and grasses gave me almost perfect cover from anyone below. Since my friendly family, however, I had met no one else on the track.

From the wild open moorland of Endecombe Moor we descended steadily past lush fields bounded by white dry stone walls, full of clean shorn sheep and their fat woolly lambs, almost as big as themselves.

I spotted the ruins of a castle as we cleared a stand of beech trees. It was standing grey and alone amid the green and the white of the fields. I wondered if we had come far enough for this to be Birkhampton. Oscar stood while I fished the map out of the saddlebag and took a look. It was Birkhampton Castle! In my scramble last night to sort out a route and get going I hadn't even noticed this. Was this a likely place for knights? I strained my eyes, but I couldn't see anything so I dug the binoculars out and had another look.

Bunting and flags suddenly jumped into focus, strung up from the battlements! Still no sign of people, they must be on the far side. Panning round there was a sudden glimmer of white. A tent! Well, it had to be the best place to start. Even if there weren't any knights here, at least someone would know.

We left the track and cut across several fields before coming to the far side of the castle. Suddenly the world was alive with people. There was a big gate, with a banner over it proclaiming 'Country Fayre and Medieval jousting by the Devil's Riders.' Of course! Jousting would have knights. Had I been fixed up with a jousting troupe? I couldn't believe my luck! Excitedly I looked for the jousters and then spotted their own banner flying from a tent at the base of the castle walls.

When I got there the camp seemed deserted. I looked round for someone then saw a small man with a pronounced limp coming out of a tent. Dismounting I led Oscar over and asked if he knew where Ron was. He looked at me sharply.

'Who wants to know?' he demanded.

'I was told to come to Ron who is with some knights, in Birkhampton, today, and that I would be able to travel with them. That's all I know . . .' I tailed off.

His face was blank.

'Ron's not here,' he said, abruptly. 'He had to go away suddenly. I don't know anything about anyone coming along for the ride. We don't do that sort of thing. People who are here, work.' He turned and started to limp away.

I didn't know what to do. The message had obviously not got to this man but I needed to convince him somehow. Pulling Oscar with me, I called out, after him, 'Wait, please. Please wait!'

He halted and turned, impatience smeared across his face.

'Well?'

'Delilah sent me,' I tried. He still looked blank.

'Are you . . . are you the round tablers?' I whispered. I was giving my secret information away, to someone I didn't know or trust. But I had to risk it.

He almost jumped into my face.

'How did you know that?' he hissed. 'I'm the only one around here who knows that. Who told you?'

'I don't know their name,' I said honestly, 'they just did.'

'What's your name?' he demanded.

'Sam,' I said. I had thought about this carefully as I had been riding along. If my parents were interrogated with truth drugs they would give the name Tamsin straightaway. Also, the man who'd ambushed me yesterday had mistaken me for a boy and that disguise might come in handy. So I had chosen the name of my hero, Samwise Gamgee in the Lord of the Rings. Faithful, courageous and a horse owner. Who better?

'Put your horse in the stable tent,' he said with a scowl. 'We're performing now. We strike at nine, move off at ten. Make yourself useful. We don't carry anyone.' He limped off.

The stable tent was just that – a tent divided up into stalls with canvas walls. It was cool and smelt of horses and sweet meadow hay. It was empty at the moment but it was obvious which of the stalls had had occupants. We found an unoccupied stall. I untacked Oscar, brushed him down and gave him a drink. Vince wanted to stretch his legs so we went out to see what was happening.

Even though the castle was a ruin, with all the banners and the colourful costumes of the knights, it provided a dramatic backdrop to the spectacular jousting of the Devil's Riders. I'd never seen such trick riding before. There were eight knights competing, the best of whom was Sir Wolfbane who rode a fizzy chestnut mare. Sir Wolfbane was the prime contender for the queen's favour. He won most of the contests so seemed set to be champion until the very last pass when a complete outsider, the Black Knight, stampeded into the ring and sent him flying, accompanied by much booing and hissing from the packed audience. The Black Knight won, accepted the cup with little grace and galloped off into the distance. I was so caught up in the performance that I would have completely believed in the Black Knight, if I hadn't seen him dismount at a distance and lead his enormous black horse back to the stable tent. Who was this Knight – what a great rider he was! I'd never be as good as the Devil's Riders. The memory of my sad efforts hit me, like a punch in the stomach, before I could control it. Me, on my trick saddle, with an old pole painted as a lance, knitted chainmail and a papier-mâché helmet made in one of my history projects. Galloping in our flattest field, Oscar trying his best to stay on all four feet over the grass tussocks, towards Vince . . .

The lovely smoky smell of a barbecue penetrated my reverie and suddenly the picnic shared with the little family seemed a long time ago. I followed my nose over to a fire where the troupe was gathering, enamel plates in hand. The barbecue had been built from some of the ancient castle stones that littered the ground. On it was an old farm riddle and the whole thing had been constructed under the awning of the stables tent. I thought this could be quite dangerous.

'Never you mind,' grunted Ron, his voice thick and juicy as the sausage sandwich he was greedily consuming, 'you'll be glad if it starts to rain.' I joined the queue and soon had my own.

I sat on a rock and tore into it, giving a share to Vince, who was looking a lot better. Everyone was friendly; no one had expressed any surprise or interest in my presence. It was almost as if I had been there forever. It hit me. Stupid! They had obviously done this before!

It was weird. I was accepted for who I was, that day, that time. Nobody wanted to know about my past, or my future. For the first time since I'd discovered my parents' abduction I felt at peace, even excited at the thought of living with these horses and riders for the next few days. I felt safe too. Nothing could touch us among this mad, horsey crowd, could it?

I asked one of the knights what was next on the plan.

'We get a kip,' he said, 'until nine.'

I took the hint.

The stable tent was now full of horses and the sound of them all rhythmically crunching their food was very soothing. Horses were obviously the priority. That was fine by me. Ron had his own reasons for his hostility to me.

Pulling my sleeping bag from the saddlebag I snuggled down in the corner of Oscar's stall. Vince flopped onto the end and we all three fell asleep. During my sleep I dreamed – or maybe it was real – that a group of people had come into the tent. Probably a dream as I heard the same words.

'We get a kip, until nine.'

Dream or reality it was nothing to do with me and effortlessly I fell back into sleep.

I woke to the bustle of striking camp. Peering at my watch I saw that I'd had four hours' sleep. I hoped Oscar had had the same. Vince was attacking an enormous bowl of food. Who had put that there for him? Whoever it was understood a working dog's appetite. And Oscar, come to that. Whoever heard of a horse being fed hay in the middle of summer? But he wasn't complaining. Munching away with a dreamy look in his eye, as if to say, these people really know how to look after a horse.

'Hi Sam, slept enough?' It was Ron.

For a fraction of a second, coming out of sleep I couldn't work out who he meant. With a big effort I dragged myself into consciousness and remembered.

'Fine, thank you,' I said. And got up to help with the packing. This had obviously been done hundreds of times before and was so well organised that everything was packed and stowed in an hour. Everybody had their own tasks. All I could do was make sure we three were ready and not in anyone's way. Someone had even made cold sausage sandwiches from the barbecue. A tasty supper – or was it breakfast? We all gathered round Ron, munching while he gave us instructions. He explained how the next part of the journey would be managed.

'We travel overnight because we need to cover large distances between gigs. It's also much better for the horses in the hot months – flies.'

I understood that. We often looked at the sheep

in the evenings in the summer because of the flies. And Oscar sometimes stayed in all day and went out at night on very hot days . . .

'But the main reason is that there's hardly any other traffic at night and where there's no traffic there are hardly any check points. But there is a downside. There's always a downside.'

He paused, dramatically.

'There will be SpyBirds!'

# CHAPTER 6

I looked around. Most people were ignoring Ron's talk, carrying on their own conversations. The terror those words struck in my heart was obviously not replicated in others. Was all this for my benefit then, or were there others who were new here as well?

'This is the way we travel. Two jousting horses at a time get two hours' rest in the horse wagon. Every two hours we change round. The horses pulling the wagon get a rest at our next gig, which tomorrow is at Lexmouth.' For the first time he looked straight at me. 'Your horse will have to do the same. The knights try and get some sleep with their horses – that's why they're called the Devil's Riders – always exhausted and bad-tempered. Don't wind 'em up!'

Obviously an old joke, it got one or two groans. He continued. 'There's no night curfew at the moment. But any largish group attracts attention so we break into smaller groups. They don't normally bother us like that. You go out in no less than twos, no more than fours. You go out at ten-minute intervals. If a 'Bird comes over, don't run into the nearest barn and hide – too suspicious! If you have time, slide off into a ditch. If not, just keep walking slowly. Don't react.'

I was suddenly struck. Was everyone here on the run, on the wanted list, even the knights?

Ron was coming over to me. 'Go and get that horse of yours into camouflage and get yourself a balaclava,' he muttered.

Intrigued, I found a man who was in charge of tack. He gave me some cloth covers for my stirrups to stop them glinting and a camouflage saddle cover in case I had to slide off and leave the saddle on. I had to wear a thin cotton balaclava to stop my face reflecting any light.

'What about Vince' I asked him. 'He's got lots of white bits.'

He thought for a moment. 'If he lies very still they probably won't pick him up. It's like his own camouflage jacket! Can you make him do that?'

'Hear that?' I murmured into his fur, 'do it or else we're in deep trouble, mister.'

Vince rolled over on his back. 'Not like that, silly. You've no camouflage on your tum at all!'

. . . .

The SpyBird patrol appeared six hours into the ride. We were on our third exchange and everyone was drooping with exhaustion. There was even a very faint cream tinge on the horizon. It seemed to give us a sense that our journey was almost over and we had dropped our guard a little.

But only a little. Ron's strict orders were still being adhered to and we were well spread out. Then the deafening, clattering noise of rotors burst over the high tor that we were walking by and two helicopters materialised in the sky above in what felt like microseconds.

Oscar hated helicopters and aeroplanes with a passion. At home we were the highest spot for miles. We could see the Atlantic in one direction and Endecombe Moor in the opposite and planes and helicopters regularly flew and danced over this point. They would fly as low as they could, or waggle their wings or loop the loop. They would assemble above us or come as a group and speed away from it. Mum, Dad and I would usually hide in the Pad where we were invisible.

Oscar would run. Unmounted he would gallop away as far as he could and stand quivering at the farthest boundary of his field. Ridden, he would try to bolt but these days I was usually strong enough to hold him.

But not tonight. His keen ears heard the noise before anyone else and he was off. He had spotted a gap in a dry stone wall on the other side of which was a little copse. He was through the gap almost before I had woken out of my stupor. Our companion, who was called Solo, followed in quick succession thanks to his horse who had been infected by Oscar's panic. By the time the SpyBirds were overhead, Solo, Vince and I were face down on the inside of the wall. The horses, on the end of their reins, were feeling safer under cover of the copse, which they demonstrated by starting to crop at the grass.

I was so glad that I was used to SpyBird patrols. They were so terrifying I was sure I'd have let myself down if it had been the first time. I particularly did not want to let myself down at this moment.

Solo was intriguing me. We had joined forces at the last exchange, about half an hour before. The way Ron had it organised meant that we changed riding partners at every horse exchange. This was good for a newcomer like me to get to know people. I'm sure his reasons weren't those, but I had chatted easily with my two previous companions. Fred played Sir Neville in the jousts and Lucy played his squire Rhys and was also the Devils' chief groom. But my third companion, Solo, apart from a quiet 'hello' had not uttered a word since.

It was probably the lack of conversation that had made me start to doze in the saddle. The rhythmic walking motion, the soft swish of the horses' tails and the creak of the leather tack had all been very soporific.

Now it was a very different story. We'd been literally thrown together in a shallow ditch and I could actually feel him holding his breath, like I was mine. On my other side Vince panted wetly into my neck.

The 'Birds' lights were penetrating. If we'd been in the open, the lights would have picked us up with ease. As it was, the wall gave us protection and the edge of the lights was flickering and pushing but still metres away. I wondered how the rest of the troupe was managing, especially the horse wagon. Designed to look like an old farm wagon maybe it would pass. By now on a summer's morning, many real farmers would already be up and about as well.

'I think they're going,' said Solo, so suddenly that it made me jump.

He was right. The horrible noise disappeared almost as quickly as it had arrived. We waited a bit to be sure then slowly got up and stretched – and then realised exactly what we'd been hiding in.

'Gorse,' I yelped, 'ouch!'

'And brambles,' said Solo, 'and yuk! What's this?'

'Er . . . sheep . . . poo actually,' I said, trying not to laugh.

'I heard that,' Solo said, laughing himself now. He had a nice laugh, I thought, a rich throaty chuckle.

'I think it should be safe to move on, don't you?' Solo said. I thought so too so we quickly mounted and set off again.

It was different now. We'd shared danger. The awkward uneasiness had evaporated.

Suddenly I stopped, shocked.

'Where's Vince?' I shouted.

'Shh . . . Sam,' warned Solo. 'Who's Vince?'

'He's my dog,' I said 'he was with us until the helicopters went. You must have seen him. He's a collie and he's like my shadow. He's got very sore feet. He should be up here with me. 'I was starting to panic. How could I have forgotten him? I started to turn Oscar around.

'No Sam, you can't do that,' urged Solo 'you'll get all mixed up with those following and if the 'Birds come back . . .'

Without thinking I pulled my binoculars out

of my saddlebag, switched on the infrared and clamped them to my eyes, looking in the direction we'd travelled.

'What have you got there?' asked Solo, interested, 'are they night glasses? I had to leave mine behind when . . . er . . . Can I have a look?'

I would have to be a lot more careful, I thought, but I couldn't really try and hide them now. I handed them over, still worried about Vince. Suppose he'd got stuck, or fallen down a hole . . .

'Yes, here he is,' said Solo, calmly, 'hobbling back to his daddy!'

I shot a look at him. Did he think I was a boy as well? Still, it was dark and we both had balaclavas on.

I got off and greeted Vince. Although he was still lame, he was much better. The resting and the ointment were working.

'Where've you been, you silly dog?' I chastised and hugged him at the same time. He rolled over for a tummy rub, then I carefully swung him up, once again, onto Oscar's saddle.

'How did he hurt his paws?' Solo asked.

'I don't know,' I said cagily, 'he just turned up like it'.

We looked away from each other and retreated once more into our private worlds.

When we met up with the rest of the Devils

at seven we found that we'd had a lucky escape. Others hadn't. The SpyBirds had appeared so suddenly that most of the horses had spooked. The horse wagon had gone on its side and the two poor horses inside obviously had fallen too. They were shocked and cut but fortunately nothing broken. One of the horses pulling the wagon seemed to have twisted his back so he would have to rest from work for a few days.

The most serious casualty was Fred. He'd been trying to slide off his horse when she bolted. His foot had stuck in the stirrup and he had been bumped along for several metres before managing to haul himself back on by the stirrup and stop. But his ankle had been broken and he was in severe pain. It was all strapped up but he kept losing consciousness so Ron was organising a group to take him to a horse doctor they could trust near Lexmouth. I understood about this. Loads of doctors continued to work unregistered and under the regime's radar. They called themselves smiths or horse doctors or animal practitioners.

Ron was also trying to get together a team of horses and riders who were well enough to perform in the afternoon's joust. In the end, with lots of shuffling about – a bit like a game of drafts I thought – they were one horse and rider short.

'Daren't go in with one less,' mused Ron,

thinking aloud. 'We double up anyway and we run very tight. If we sell them short the organisers will complain to the authorities and as well as not getting paid, it'll raise our profile too much. If anyone's got any good ideas how to get out of this one, let's have 'em now.'

Everyone thought again, but all the ideas had been used up. I didn't want the profile of the Riders raised – it would mean I would have to leave and at the moment it seemed to be the safest place to be. I stepped forward. Ron didn't even glance in my direction.

'I can joust,' I said nervously.

Everybody stopped talking and looked my way. A few grins appeared.

'Oh right,' Ron said rudely 'any other suggestions anybody?' The chatting recommenced.

I was angry now. 'I <u>can</u> joust,' I said fiercely, 'watch me!'

I had hold of Oscar's reins and I swung up on him. Vince limped after me and I told him firmly to lie flat and stay. I squeezed Oscar into canter, then gallop and travelled for about a twenty five metres before turning. I could see I had everyone's attention now. I felt sick. How stupid, how arrogant I was! Who was I, a tin pot little rider who'd only ever jousted in a farm field, thinking I was good enough?

'Charge!' I said to Oscar. That was the beauty of this horse. I only had to say what I wanted and he'd do it. He charged.

My beautiful trick saddle was no more. Never mind, I'd manage without. I'd done that lots of times. I took one foot out of the irons and twisted it through the stirrup leather. We were bearing down on Vince. Poor dog had his head down, prepared for me to reach down and snatch something from his collar except there was nothing to snatch. Never mind, I'd improvise. I'd done that, lots of times as well. I'd worked myself into such a fury by now, I only noticed at the last second that somebody had dropped a cowboy hat on the ground for me to retrieve.

Slipping my other foot out of the irons I slid all the way down, hanging on tightly to the stirrup leather, to where the hat was. Oscar never faltered in his gallop even though his centre of gravity was being seriously disturbed. Snatching the hat I was back up, not very elegantly, but secure. Through the pounding in my head I could hear applause. I pushed the hat securely on.

'Slow down,' I commanded Oscar. He slowed his gallop right down so that I could swing both legs over to land lightly on one side, then vault back up and over to the other. I had only ever done the next thing with my trick saddle – but the adrenalin was up and they were still clapping! I got to my feet and stood on the saddle while Oscar slowed it to a steady canter, then a walk, then halted. The applause died away.

Ron limped up to us. He smiled! There were a few broken teeth in there but it was much better than the scowl.

'He can joust,' he said.

# CHAPTER 7

'Right,' said Ron, briskly, 'come with me.' He put his arm round my shoulders and took me to one side of the stable tent. 'Get yourself a proper haircut,' he said quietly. 'You're going to be Sir Robert of Lothian. Knights and curls don't mix.'

Did he know then? It had been a while since I'd had a cut and it had got a bit bushy. In fact there'd been a haircut scheduled for the night of the fire . . .

He was glaring at me again.

'Go with Lucy now please,' he said gruffly and he went off to inspect his battered little army.

'I don't know why he thinks I'll do a good job,' laughed Lucy. 'Probably to do with me clipping out and trimming manes and tails. Come on. Lets see what we can do.'

Of course it reminded me of hairdressing

sessions with Mum, relaxed, chatty. To change that subject in my head I asked her,

'Where do we go to next? Do you know?'

There was a fraction's hesitation before she answered.

'We're going to Carding next, then Hanvil, then I believe we're heading north, up country. Ron keeps it all in that busy head of his. Why do you want to know, Sam?'

It was so comfortable, so warm in this corner of the stables that I almost blurted out,

'Because I want to know if we're anywhere near where they've taken my parents!' Instead I said lamely,

'Just wondered. Never travelled much before.'

Lucy laughed. 'I think I can safely say you've got plenty of travelling ahead of you with the Devil's Riders! Now, howzat?' She handed me a cracked mirror from the costume trunk.

I couldn't believe it. She'd done such a good job that even I didn't recognise myself!

Solo came to help me groom and turn Oscar into a gleaming jousting horse.

'Didn't you want to ride this afternoon?' I asked him. 'I feel awful just turning up. .'

'I can't trick ride,' Solo replied. 'and I only joined the Devils yesterday.'

I glanced at him from my side as I was brushing Oscar. So had I but I couldn't remember him being around when I first came. When had he arrived? Was it when I was asleep? Perhaps it hadn't been a dream after all. I had only seen his face for the first time just an hour before, when we had both unmasked. It was broad with a snub nose and freckles. He had twinkling green eyes and a shock of dead straight gingery blond hair, like a brush. My dad has hair like that, I thought with a painful memory rush.

There always seemed to be a gleam of mischief lurking in Solo's eyes, or just around his mouth. But an honest face, I thought. I would have loved his straight hair. My curls always looked such a mess. Except now . . . my hand strayed to my head. I wasn't used to the lightness.

'It suits you,' he grinned, 'I prefer it to before.' Then he surprised me by going bright red! He ducked down on his side.

'I think Lucy can only do short or extremely short with the horse clippers! Anyway, at least my helmet won't keep falling off like it does at home!' I said.

'And where's home?' Solo's voice was slightly muffled, his face half buried in Oscar's side as he reached to brush his stomach.

'In . . .'I started but Oscar stamped. He wasn't

keen on stomach grooming. 'Don't worry, I'll do his tum.' I stood up and straightened my back. Then I remembered what the mother of the red headed children had said, the day before. 'The less I know, the less I can tell.' I certainly did not want to endanger a friend and I found myself hoping that this boy with the ready laugh would be a very good friend.

'I live in the south,' I said. Not quite the truth but not wholly a lie. 'What about you, Solo?'

'Oh, all over the place. Where are you going?'

'Oh, just visiting relatives,' I said, lamely.

'Isn't it a bit risky on your own? Why didn't one of your parents come with you?'

'I'm fourteen!' I said indignantly. 'And I'm fine. They're farmers you see, don't have time . . .' Suddenly, I was very pleased to have found a stubborn bit of mud just under Oscar's armpit. I had just been reminded of why I was here. The task ahead was huge and here I was, about to blurt out the whole story to a complete stranger! When would I ever learn to control my mouth?

I took a quick look at Solo, but he was unconcerned, brushing away on his side.

Oscar was ready now. It was still three hours to go to the show and we all badly needed a rest. Grabbing a horse blanket each, we rolled up in them and lay down on a bed of straw bales in the back of the stable tent, Vince between us.

I sat on Oscar, perfectly still. At the other end of the tilt sat Sir Oswald, resplendent in royal blue plumage and tabard, on his dappled grey. Although I loved my (slightly round) piebald cob with all my heart, in the present company of fine jousting horses I had to admit, he was out of his league in the looks department.

However he could do his stuff. And we had practised the next bit hundreds of times at home.

But never in front of an audience of more than two before.

I felt sick.

What if Oscar stumbled – he sometimes did – and I came tumbling off before I was meant to? What if . . . ?

I snapped my mind back to my orders. We were both to 'miss' the first pass and the second I was to fall off and Sir Oswald was to win. Then I had to make my way back to the tent and get out of costume, out of sight.

I was privately hoping to catch the Black Knight robing up. I hadn't seen him at all during the day but his horse was there, all tacked up and ready to go. I had a good idea who he was. Or thought I did . . .

The silk handkerchief fell. We were off. All I had to do was to ride straight and stay on. We galloped past each other, crashing our lances noisily but sitting tight.

I was thinking that half of it was over, only the fall to come, when there was a roar behind me which turned into loud boos and hisses. There was a crack of lances and I looked, just in time to see Sir Oswald flying through the air after being hit by the Black Knight! Now where had he come from? He'd broken all the rules by attacking at the end of the tilt, but of course that was all part of the act and the crowd loved it.

But it was not in my script. I'd reached the end of the tilt and was circling round. What on earth was I supposed to do now?

The Black Knight gave me no time to worry as he was already on his way towards me at full gallop. I'd just have to play it by ear and see what happened. I squeezed Oscar forward and off we went.

Therwack! The Black Knight's lance hit me across the shoulder and sent me spinning. I had no choice. Managing half a break fall I landed heavily on my back, winded. I lay there, struggling to get my breath back. Solo, who was acting as my squire, ran over to help me up.

'Are you all right?' he asked in a concerned voice, 'that was a bit over the top!'

I still couldn't speak, but let him lead me away.

My mind was spinning as much as my body had been. For the Black Knight had shouted 'Delilah, stay with the Devils!' before knocking me off Oscar.

And the voice that had shouted was high pitched and shrill.

The Black Knight had been a woman!

# CHAPTER 8

We were famished. Our day had been all over the place, getting Fred to the doctor's to have his ankle set, patching up horses and trying to keep the show on the road in between.

Ron had given in to pressure and allowed us to go to the hog roast as long as we were not in costume and didn't all go together.

'You can go if you like,' he said to me. 'It looks safe enough. Keep your eyes down, don't make eye contact, but walk as if you know where you're going. Anything suspicious, leg it back here and jump in the hay!'

I nodded and followed him. I hadn't seen him since the jousting and I was dying to ask him a question.

'Ron, who plays the Black Knight?'

He gave me a sideways glance. 'Sometimes it's

one of us. Sometimes someone comes along who wants a ride. Who wants to know?'

I shrugged. No help there then.

But Ron also had something to say. He checked all round first.

'While I've got you on your own. Don't know yer history, don't know yer plans. Don't want to. The less I know . . .'

'. . . the less you can give away,' I finished for him. He grunted.

'That's right. But whatever happens, if the worst happens, don't you worry about me, or the Riders – giving us away. We'll disappear just like that and we'll pop up again somewhere else – different names, different show. We've done it lots of times before and we'll do it again. It's all part of the job. Understand?'

I didn't, but it was the longest speech I'd ever heard from Ron so I nodded. He seemed satisfied and grunted again.

In my head I was puzzling away at the Black Knight. It was obvious someone wanted to get a message to me, but how had they known I would be riding? It had only been decided that morning. So was it someone from the Riders? But all the trick riders were men! I had a quick look round but of course no one was looking in my direction at all. It felt spooky – or comforting. I didn't quite know which.

The mouth-watering smell of roasting pork was becoming stronger with every step. As we approached the stall Solo caught up with me. He'd been running.

'What do you want?' he panted.

'A large pork bap with everything please.' My stomach was rumbling just at the thought of it. 'But I'm sorry. I've no money.'

'Don't worry about that,' he laughed, ' in a few days you can pay me back. As a han'some knight you'll get money thrown at you!'

'Who by?' I was intrigued.

'All the pretty girls of course'.

This was starting to feel surreal. I followed him and we settled in the back of the stables tent and hungrily attacked our hog roast baps. We didn't say one more thing until we'd eaten every last juicy, fragrant mouthful. Exhausted, we flopped back against the straw bale. We rested in companionable silence for a while.

'Did you hear what the Black Knight shouted at you, Sam?' suddenly asked Solo, out of the gloom.

'Not really,' I mumbled, surprised. 'Did you?'

'No. But why did he shout, do you think?'

'Haven't a clue,' I said truthfully. I didn't have a clue, but also I wanted him to drop it. It was my problem and I would have to solve it somehow. But there was something I wanted to know.

'You know them a bit by now. Was the Black Knight one of the Riders?' I asked.

'I didn't see,' Solo replied, 'I was too busy helping you up. I think they all take it in turns.'

'Where's his horse kept?'

'In the tent, like all the others,' he replied. He looked at me for a second. 'You're a superb rider, Sam. I wish I could ride like that. My mother can trick ride just like you, she just doesn't get the chance these days!'

I was blushing madly, but full of questions too. Then . . .

'Where are those lazy lads?' Ron was shouting. Quickly jumping to our feet we went to help strike camp. I found myself eagerly looking forward to my next ride with Solo.


We had picked up Fred from the outskirts of Lexmouth with his leg in a splint and 'off his head' with painkillers according to Alex, another knight. Fred had to travel in the horse wagon. He would need those painkillers – it was a jolting uncomfortable ride for anyone. The horse that had twisted his back was still not fit to drive and they needed a horse to stand in. I volunteered Oscar as he could both ride and drive so Vince and I journeyed the next leg to the market town of Carding Norton, squashed up alongside Alex on the driver's bench. Alex drove smoothly, so with the warmth and the regular soft beat of the horses' hooves on the grassy roads, I dozed a fair bit of the way. Once I jolted awake to find Alex's head on my shoulder, the reins loose in his lap while the horses maintained their pace, without supervision. He yawned when I gently nudged him awake.

'I don't think they really need me, do you Sam?' he laughed.

Suddenly, near the end of the journey again, danger!

It was still dark but the horses' heads were visible in the starlight. Both their ears shot forward.

'Something ahead,' Alex whispered. He was straining to see, slowing as a precaution. I had a look with my night glasses.

'There's some people,' I whispered, 'and they've put a pole across the road!'

'A road block! Get back Sam. They'll be doing retinal scans! Hide under Fred's blankets!'

As smoothly as I could, in case they had glasses on me, I turned and made my way into the trailer. It was hard not to fall over – we were bumping along an overgrown track and felt every clod of hardened earth.

Fred was snoring away regardless. He had thrown all his blankets off – it was a hot night. I knew a thin sheet would not hide me. We were slowing right down now and I could hear voices calling us to stop. Frantically I looked for somewhere to go. I stumbled into the back where the two horses were. I could hear them crunching hay, unconcerned at my presence. We had decided that it was too hot for their rugs and had folded them up in the corner of each stall. There were two half-pole dividers down the length of the trailer, one above the other, separating the horses and preventing them from banging against each other. I grabbed a rug and put it over me, then straddled the lower pole, lying along it and hoping I looked like a lumpy rug and that my feet were invisible in the straw.

As soon as I lay down along the pole the heat stifled me. The pole dug into me, all along my body, so I could feel a pain, so hot it must be dividing me in two. Surely I couldn't hold this position for long enough!

Voices were coming closer. They must have climbed in through the front like I had done. Had they seen me after all? I held my breath.

'What's in there?' I saw a flicker of torchlight through the end of the rug. It swept all round.

'Two horses and all our equipment.' Alex's voice.

'Can I go down?' the other voice said.

'Of course, just be careful of the one on the left, he's got a nasty set of teeth, and the other one has a vicious kick,' replied Alex, helpfully. The horses didn't seem to care about the lies. They carried on munching hay.

'I can get them out for you if you like,' Alex continued. 'It'll take about twenty minutes – there's all our tent and everything stowed in there...'

There was silence and for a moment I thought he was going to call Alex's bluff.

'I don't suppose anyone'll be there if there's a lot of kicking and biting . . .' and the voice receded and the light went out. I breathed again. And waited.

The light flicked on again.

'Could've sworn there were two of you when I looked from the roadblock.'

So he had seen me!

'Could've been the dog I suppose.' Alex again, quick as a flash. He'd done this before. It was obvious.

The light flicked off again. After a few moments I felt the trailer start again. It was agony but I wasn't going to move until Alex said so. After what seemed like hours he called me. I peeled myself off the pole and stood upright on trembling legs and rubbed my sore body. I was convinced I would have a black and blue line all down my front.

Once again I sent a silent 'thank you' to my parents for all they'd taught me. As I made my way forward I wondered how Solo had managed. I had a strong suspicion he wouldn't have wanted that scan either.

And was I being paranoid, or was it more than a coincidence, that our little troupe, spread out on scarcely used byways had now been targeted on two consecutive nights?

# CHAPTER 9

We started pitching camp as soon as we arrived at the site at Carding Norton. The Riders were arriving in their groups of twos and threes but no sign of Solo. We were all involved in the work so I hadn't time to worry. I did start to when he still hadn't appeared by the end of the next hour.

Nearly two hours later I was leading Oscar into his tent stall for a well-deserved breakfast, convinced that I would never see Solo again. When he wearily walked round the corner of the stable tent I was so relieved I had to stop myself from running over and hugging him.

He gave me a tired grin but said there had been no sign of a roadblock when they had come through. He and Lucy had been the last pair, that's why he was so late.

Once the horses were fed, watered and settled

we could do the same. I had an apple for breakfast before making my bed with Vince in the corner of Oscar's stall.

We had two shows to perform that afternoon. This time I had a little more understanding of what was going on and was a bit more relaxed. No Black Knight appeared so Oscar and I were finished quite quickly and with honour. We had been allowed to topple Sir Oswald in the second show and then Oscar went back to the stable tent to continue his sleep.

In the queue for another hog roast – would I ever get tired of them I wondered? – I sought out Solo. Now I was here, I suddenly felt shy. But I did need his help.

'Could we ride together tonight?' I asked him. I could feel myself blushing. He gave me a quick look and a smile.

'I was going to suggest the same thing. Then we can talk about what the Black Knight said!'

But I had something much more important to tell him.

We had chosen to ride the first leg together and we went at a fast walk, sensing the sun disappear to the west, behind us, losing its warmth. We talked companionably about the day, our constant state of exhaustion and our wish for something green in our diet. Then we both fell silent. On my part it was from nervousness. I didn't really know how to start. I was glad of the darkening sky. At least my red face wouldn't be so noticeable.

'Er . . . Solo,' I started.

'Sam,' he said at exactly the same moment.

We both laughed, nervously.

'You go,' he insisted, 'you were first.'

I wasn't but I went anyway. I focussed on Oscar's ears.

'Solo, I like you very much and I want to tell you that I'm . . . I'm a girl!'

Silence. Horrible. One that you could cut with a sword. I took a peep sideways.

In the gloom a whole series of emotions seemed to be passing over Solo's face. Surprise, disappointment, then something rising from his throat which – turned into a howl of laughter!

My embarrassment was changing to anger. He noticed and put his hand on my arm. Funnily enough I hadn't taken any notice of his hands before. They were strong, but small and neat. Almost dainty . . .

'Sam, I like you very much too and I . . . I'm a girl as well!' At this he/she had hysterics and almost fell off her horse. Once I'd got over my surprise I joined in. For the next twenty minutes we alternated between screaming with laughter and silent intervals when we suddenly remembered how we'd felt about each other up until —well, just now.

'Oh I'm so embarrassed,' laughed Solo after one of these pauses. 'I'm so sad. The first person I really get to know properly and I think I'm in love!'

'You're not sad,' I said, 'I think we must have led very sheltered lives.'

'So sheltered we can't even tell the difference between a boy and a girl,' she gasped – and we were off again.

Our stomachs ached and our voices were hoarse by the time we came to our senses and remembered that we should be keeping 'as quiet and invisible as we could' as per Ron's instructions. And, most importantly I now knew I could trust my new companion with everything.

'Shall we talk about the Black Knight,' I suggested, mopping at the tears coursing down my face, 'maybe it'll take our minds off . . . off. .this!'

She nodded and we walked apart for a bit until we had regained control of our breathing.

'I did hear what he said,' I confessed, 'and by the way, he was a she as well!' We looked at each other. Somehow this wasn't as funny as before. Solo shrugged, puzzled.

'The Black Knight gave me the message *stay*

*with the Devils!'* I continued 'Or, to put it another way, don't leave!'

'Leave to go where?' Solo asked, reasonably.

'Haven't a clue,' I said truthfully. 'I've never travelled. All my geography's been learnt from our globe at home and by starting from different places and orienteering back home with a map and compass. They were very good lessons,' I added, thinking of the other night, getting to Birkhampton.

'Have you got them now? Your map and compass I mean,' asked Solo.

'Of course. Never travel without. Why?'

'I'm just wondering . . . maybe the Riders are going to, or near somewhere you're not supposed to.'

I wasn't really following her but I didn't have a better suggestion. We paused under some trees, while I fished out the map. Vince's back formed a convenient cushion to spread it over.

'Now we're heading for Hanvil tonight,' said Solo, 'so let's look at the general direction. If we sort of draw a line through where we've been and carry it on, always assuming we're taking the shortest route.' She bent over the map with the torch carefully shielded. She sucked in her breath sharply.

'That's it! That must be it,' she said softly.

'What is?' I peered over, trying to see what she had.

'Newchester. Someone doesn't want you to go to Newchester.'

'How do you know?'

Looking at me gravely she said, 'Have you never heard of it? It's called the Prison City! The prison is huge. It was built round the old castle. It's said half a million people are locked up there. Half a million! A city in a city. All the dissidents and political prisoners. All the people who oppose the regime. Didn't you know that?'

I shook my head. How was I ever going to find my parents in half a million?

Solo straightened up and looked at me. In the moonlight her eyes were black. 'It's where people are tortured and truth drugs are used. It's the most heavily guarded prison in the country: they've rebuilt the old Roman walls . . .' She tailed off and I could see tears glittering in her eyes. My throat suddenly felt as dry as ash and I shivered.

'Why would someone think you'd want to go to Newchester?' she asked, thoughtfully.

'I didn't know I did, until just now,' I answered. ' But you're right. I do have to go there. But how do you know so much about it? And why are you so upset?'

'Because my parents have been captured and are almost certainly being held there,' said Solo. 'It's where I've got to go to, as well!'

93

# CHAPTER 10

Solo's parents were dissidents like mine. They had fled from the regime just before Solo was born, like mine. They had evaded the enemy for fourteen years until they had been captured two weeks ago and taken away by SpyBird. But there the similarities ended. Her parents had been very important, she didn't know in what way, but they were high on the wanted list. It meant they were continually on the run, moving every two or three months between safe houses, all over the country. There was lots of support from the Tube, but for security reasons people were always changing and so she could never make friends with anyone for long. It was just Solo and her parents.

'I've always loved riding,' she said. We were well into our stride again. 'But I've never been able to have my own horse, with always having to move on. So I've just ridden anything that's around at the time. That's why I'm really jealous of you having Oscar,' she said, patting his neck. 'You can only do what <u>you</u> do if you build up a relationship with a horse. That's what Mum says. She used to have her own horse. She still misses him, she says.'

'Don't do yourself down,' I said quickly, 'you're a pretty good rider yourself. That's probably because you've ridden all sorts. I've never ridden anyone else. Probably make a mess of it.'

She looked pleased. 'Thank you,' she said. Then she giggled. 'Can you keep a secret?'

'What? Another one? Try me!'

With one hand, she twiddled her fingers near her throat. In the flickering moonlight I thought I could see something appear there. I bent forward to see better.

'Can you see her?' asked Solo and suddenly there was a small black and white creature in her hand. She placed it on the saddle pommel. It started to groom itself.

'Meet Rosemary, my rat,' Solo grinned. Having never seen a rat other than the brown ones that prowled our boundary at home, I didn't know quite how to feel.

'Where's she been?' I asked incredulously, 'I've never seen her.'

'She stays close,' explained Solo. 'And when it's

safe I let her out. I've had her for five years and believe me we've been through it. Sometimes I've had to let her go, but she always finds me again.' Picking the creature up she kissed its whiskery nose. 'Until I met you, she's been my only friend besides my mum and dad.'

I could understand that – although my particular friends were a lot bigger. I glanced at Vince – what would he think of a rat, even though it was black and white? His tail flapped, then he was back in dreamland. Hopefully we could all be friends and help each other when we went into Newchester.

Unlike me, Solo had always known of the Prison City. Her parents had made no secret of it. Many of their friends and family had been incarcerated there, some even killed, like her grandparents. So when she had returned home after a walk with Rosemary and watched with horror her parents being bundled into a SpyBird, she felt certain they would be taken there.

'How did you end up with the Devil's Riders?' I asked.

'The local Tube members fixed it up with Ron,' she said. 'They've got to arrange a new safe house somewhere and they thought this would be the best place to be while they got it sorted. The Riders are always on the move and no-one here except Ron actually knows where they're going more than one or two days ahead. Y'know, I'd no idea we were going anywhere near Newchester? I'm completely disorientated at the moment,' she added.

I nodded sympathetically.

'How did you get here? Did you ride?' I asked.

'No, I was marched here by three Tube members. We were supposed to be a small platoon. We marched at night.

'I saw you!' I exclaimed. 'I was on a bridge and you marched underneath! Was Ron expecting you? He definitely wasn't me!'

'I don't think so,' Solo said, 'but it's all happened so quickly, for everyone.'

'And what were your instructions,' I asked curiously. 'Surely they don't expect you to go in and try to rescue them singlehanded?'

'You must be joking! I mustn't even think about it!' She mimicked how her orders had been delivered. 'They would have people ready to move in immediately, trained, equipped . . . and all that stuff. In other words, stay where you are and we'll take care of everything.'

'Funny that – my instructions were the same. Then the Black Knight came along and said it again,' I said.

We looked at each other.

'How could they possibly think I would just sit around like a . . . a . . .'

'A bowl of soup?' I supplied.

'Like a bowl of soup, waiting for someone else to do it,' she went on, indignation building, 'they must have known I'd want to go and find them! So I'm going anyway. And now I've met you! What say you, brave knight? Two heads and two brave hearts are better than one, yes?'

I suddenly had difficulty breathing, my throat was so tight. What if it was too late? What if our parents were already dead? I daren't share these thoughts with Solo. In the face of her courage and optimism I couldn't risk acting like a wimp.

So we shook hands on it and started to plan. By the time that leg was completed we'd agreed our next step. We would be told the next stop at supper. If it would take us nearer to Newchester we'd stay with the Riders another day. If they changed direction, then we'd make our move and leave them during the next night's travel. But how were we going to be able to get into a heavily guarded city with reinforced Roman walls? We would have to leave that tricky question until later.

It was time to part for the next leg of the journey as the troupe headed towards Hanvil.

Once again I found myself in the hog roast queue and yes, I had decided that I could live on hog roast forever. When you've done a long day's work and haven't eaten since breakfast and your stomach's rumbling like thunder, a sizzling smoky hog roast feels like the perfect answer every time. Solo and I were waiting for food with Ron.

'We'll have a bit more chance to get you jousting, Solo,' he was saying. 'Fred's nowhere near riding yet, but he can groom, which frees Lucy up to ride.' He jerked his thumb at me. 'You can start to teach him a few of your tricks.' Then to Solo. 'If you listen to him, you could probably have a little part by next week.'

I glanced at Solo. Although she was blushing with pleasure at his promise, she'd be frustrated she wouldn't be able to do it. We'd be off by next week.

Something else was niggling, what was it? But I couldn't think on an empty stomach.

We stepped up, so close that our mouths were watering. We could see the steam, smell the crispy crackling.

Alex appeared silently at Ron's side.

'There's a patrol here on the lookout,' he said urgently, with a quick glance at Solo and me. 'They're spreading out, mixing with the crowds — stealth tactics.'

Ron spun round and limped away so quickly we were trotting to keep up. Goodbye to food then. But the hunger had turned to the familiar sick feeling of dread.

'How did you find out?' Ron was asking.

'Lucy heard them,' replied Alex. 'They parked up behind our tent. Four of them. The leader said to pick up anyone suspicious and ask questions later.'

He broke away. 'I'm going to head back,' he said and disappeared.

'Great,' Ron muttered, 'parked just behind us. We'll just have to be extra careful that's all and you'll have to be extra quiet.'

'Who do you think they're after?' Solo gasped. We were almost galloping at a walk by now.

'Haven't a clue! It's not unusual to find them at these sorts of events. They seem to attract misfits. Like us!'

We entered the stable tent from under one of the rolled up sides. As soon as Oscar saw me, he whinnied his greeting.

Ron rolled his eyes. 'For heavens sake,' he hissed, 'put a bandage round it!' He beckoned us to follow him and after checking there were no observers led us into the horse wagon. It was already backed up against the entrance of the tent ready to be loaded. He took us through the stall to the front. He lifted the lid on a long bench, which ran from side to side. It was full of costumes. He started to pull them out.

'There's a false bottom to this box,' he whispered, 'hop in and try to keep very still. There are some air holes drilled out underneath so you'll be able to breathe. Stay put until someone comes for you.' He dug into his pocket and took out two grimy horse carrots.

'Here, take these,' he said, 'might be the last chance you get to eat today. Sorry.' He pushed us none too gently into the space where we could just lie, full length, back to back. The lid went on and we could hear the costumes being thrown back on top.

Something moved near my neck. I started a scream, but Solo hissed,

'Sam, it's Rosemary! It's all right!'

Of course I'd completely forgotten about her and she was only finding a bit of space. I started to stroke her and my heart stopped pounding. Always a bit claustrophobic, anything to distract me from this cramped little hole was welcome.

Nothing happened for ages and I think we were even starting to doze a bit. Even though we were starving and our stomachs were rumbling in unison, it had been another long tiring day.

Suddenly there was a noise. Right underneath our ears! We were awake instantly and then I recognised it. It was Vince, whining. He must have smelt us through the air holes. If anyone sees him there I thought, they'll know I'll be nearby.

But now there were voices. Very close. I guessed whoever it was must be standing at the back of the wagon.

'Oh please please Vince, shut up,' I willed him.

The voices were too muffled to identify but the words were clear enough.

'There are no girls travelling with the Riders except the groom, Lucy.'

'You sure?'

'Course I'm sure! Think I wouldn't know the difference between a girl 'n a boy?'

'What about anyone new joining you?'

'You're joking! There's always people joining – wanting free passage, to join the circus, to run away. I never ask. Don't get into trouble that way.'

'You'll get into trouble if we find them and they've no ID.'

'Whatever. You finished? I've got work to do.'

Ron, I assumed it was Ron, stomped away. There was silence. Then a new voice. Lighter, higher. A woman's.

'I can't find them anywhere. Someone must have warned them and they're hiding.'

'Your lame friend says there's no girls.'

'I haven't noticed.'

There was an explosion of crude laughter.

'Tell you what, I'm glad I'm not in this circus

or whatever it is. All this riding – makes it so you can't tell a girl from a boy?'

The cackling stopped as quickly as it had started. 'Where're they hiding then? Have you had a look in this cart?'

They meant the wagon. We held our breath. We could hear them climbing up the ramp, their steps coming forward. They were close enough to touch us, if they had only known it. I could hear the lid of the costume box being lifted and the clothes being pulled about. It went very quiet. Could they hear our hungry stomachs? Or our pounding hearts? The lid banged down, the steps receded. We exhaled very slowly.

But then there was a scampering noise and a savage growl and . . . pandemonium!

'What the hell . . .' 'What is it?' 'It's a . . . get down you . . . ow, ouch it got my . . .' 'Take that, you dirty little . . .'

There was a thump and a terrible howl of pain. I could hardly contain myself. What had they done to Vince? Brave but stupid dog! If only he'd kept quiet!

'Who's this dog belong to? Obviously not you, the way it went for you like that!'

The woman's voice again. 'No. It's probably got lost. I've never seen it before.'

'It must belong to them. They must be here

somewhere. OK. Let's have the heat seeker. We'll soon flush 'em out.'

An infrared detector, which would map out the heat of our bodies as easily as my night glasses could pick out a deer.

It was over.

# CHAPTER 11

'They're here!' came the expected discovery. Soon we were being roughly hauled to our feet and dragged out. 'Thanks,' said one of the soldiers to someone's retreating back as they quickly hurried away. In the gloom of the tent I couldn't tell who it was. I wondered if Solo knew. How could we warn Ron, that he had a spy in his camp? Anybody he gave cover to would be at risk. Desperately I looked around, but the tent was deserted.

'C'mon you two, let's get you to the castle. They'll soon find out why you're so keen to hide.'

Marching us roughly out of the tent and through some trees into a clearing, we found ourselves facing a SpyBird, rotors slowly turning!

The fear of being spotted by one of these dreadful machines had been part of my whole life and I felt sick with dread as at last I saw one so close. Somehow, though, hearing the noise and feeling its vibrations made me realise it was just a machine. Paradoxically, mixed with the dread was a quiver of excitement. My first ever helicopter ride! I glanced at Solo, but she was giving nothing away.

As we approached the 'Bird, its rotors started to spin faster and I could feel the wind from them pressing harder and harder down onto my bare head. Hands pushed us over the threshold and we half rolled, half fell through the doorway onto the floor of the machine. Other hands grabbed at us and dragged us in and, while rising, strapped us in, back to back.

The noise was deafening. Everyone else had some sort of ear protection covering half their heads. I didn't think I would ever be able to hear again properly. We lifted vertically and then banked and it was only then that I could see we had cleared the trees. The marquees and flags soon disappeared as we gained height and we thundered and rattled on our way. Leaning into Solo's back I felt her respond. We could do this!

The flight was over in minutes. Soon we seemed to be dropping out of the sky. My stomach felt as though it had been left up there.

Our descent slowed and the noise became even louder, if that was possible. The SpyBird landed, bouncing until it was stable. The rotors slowed, then stopped. Silence. Heaven. For a moment.

'Out yer get. Wot yer waiting for?'

We were kicked and thrown out of the door. Still bound together, we had no control over our movements and we rolled and bumped together, hurting each other, powerless not to.

The two guards watched and cruelly laughed. But they soon got tired of our clownish attempts to walk in a straight line and decided to separate us. As the binding tape was ripped off, I started to pull free, desperate to massage my tingling hands.

One of the guards suddenly let out a scream. Blood was pouring from one of his hands. It looked as though he had lost part of a finger. The other one left me and ran over to help. I didn't know what was going on but then noticed Solo quietly backing away from the action. She caught my eye and beckoned me to do the same.

It seemed we had landed on top of the castle. No need to breach the walls after all! Surrounding us on all sides were the battlements. While one soldier screamed and the other one tried to stench the blood, we hopped through a space and out of sight.

Crouching behind the shelter of the parapet I quizzed Solo about what had caused such a severe wound. No hidden knife, just a set of razor teeth belonging to an innocent looking Rosemary! Solo stuck her back inside her shirt.

'Gave us the diversion we needed,' she muttered, unrepentant of the damage Rosemary had caused. 'Now let's see what we can do.'

'Let's get down and out of sight as fast as we can, first.' I was moving as I spoke.

Below us was a jumble of rooftops, guttering, even some short ladders, which should give us a way down.

'We really want to be on the inside, not the outside,' fretted Solo, as we descended.

'There's probably a way we can get in from here' I said, 'castles have to be serviced like any other building.'

Sure enough, after scrambling and sliding down some slate roofs, we came across a piece of flat roof in the middle of which were some large fans and, in its own housing, a door. There was no knob, or handle.

'Access from the inside out,' said Solo quietly.

'We'd better wait then,' I said. 'At least there are lots of hiding places.'

Solo wanted to carry on and look for another access point. In the end we compromised. We'd wait half an hour then move off. We hid round the back of one of the fans, sat down and rested.

Our plan was rewarded in minutes when,

without warning, the door was flung open and two people came out. We crouched down as low as we could and tried to breathe very quietly. I recognised the wide leather belts they had on. At home we each had one – they were for carrying tools about. Mechanics of some sort then, heads down, no conversation. Moving slowly towards one of the fan hoods they gave it a good look, then one of them took out an enormous spanner and gave something a whack. There was a huge blast of air and the fan burst into roaring life. It was so noisy now that we didn't need to worry about breathing.

Or about the noise we made chasing after the two, who hadn't said a word to each other and were now slowly making their way back to the door. We grabbed one each round the neck from behind and brought them down backwards, giving them no chance to see us. They were in some sort of uniform so we tied their hands with their neckerchiefs and we were on our way to the door. Provided the fan kept going after its crude repair, no-one would hear them if they did start shouting. At the moment they showed no sign of that, lying quietly and unresisting.

We were halfway through the door when I had a thought. It sometimes happens. I stopped. Solo looked at me impatiently. I beckoned her back.

'Uniforms', I said.

'What about them?' Solo couldn't wait to get started.

'What if everybody has them?' I pursued. 'We'd stand out a bit, yes?'

She looked at me, then herself.

'A bit,' she grinned. Although not in the colourful garments of knight and squire, our own scruffy, dirty clothes reeking of horse would have loudly advertised us anywhere.

'Stripping time then,' Solo said and walked purposefully over to the two passive mechanics. I let her go first – I'd never undressed a man before! Had she done this before, I wondered as I followed nervously. But I needn't have worried because we immediately discovered that both of them were women. Quickly and methodically we took off their dull green tops and trousers and put them on. I strapped on a tool belt and indicated to Solo to do the same. A heavyweight spanner might come in useful for all sorts of things. The mechanics were lying quietly, putting up no fight. It was very strange.

Until through the door burst three fully armed uniformed guards. Somehow our mechanics must have sounded an alarm. They swiftly assessed the situation and raised their weapons. The mechanics now shouted but uselessly against the fan noise while Solo and I walked quickly towards the door, gave the three guards a thumbs up 'thank you' and ran.

Once in we immediately moderated our steps to the slow but purposeful pace we had observed from our mechanics.

We had made it, into the ancient Castle of Newchester, the biggest prison in the most heavily guarded city in the country!

My instinct about uniforms had been right. Everywhere, people in all kinds of uniform, some very smart, some workmanlike, but all in that same dull green, walked purposefully but slowly along vast, wide corridors. No-one glanced in our direction. In fact, no-one looked anywhere but down. With the number on the move it was surprising there weren't multiple pile-ups all the time. No-one talked either and although there was the sound of hundreds of feet treading the grey slate floors, the sound of anyone talking would surely have echoed in the vaulted space above us, which looked like it followed the original castle roof lines.

It was impossible for us not to talk. We didn't have a plan: we didn't know where we were. So when we wanted to speak we gently collided, then made for the nearest fire exit. Here we had a whispered discussion then pushed back into the corridors. It was during these asides that I learnt about lifts and how to tell which floor we were on.

'You have lived a sheltered life,' said Solo drily at one point.

'A very free life, actually,' I said primly. 'Anyway how come you know so much about castles and things?' I quizzed.

'Only buildings with stairs and lifts.' She was amused.

On another of our little chats, we decided to ditch the leather belts.

'I'm getting attached to this wrench,' I admitted ruefully.

'I know, but now they've found those women the first thing they'll look for is anyone with a leather belt. How many others have you seen?'

'None,' I agreed. 'But I'm going to keep the screwdriver. So should you.' Mum had taught me how to turn one into an effective weapon if I was attacked.

'Agreed,' said Solo and we carefully disposed of the belts down a rubbish chute in a wall.

Ten minutes later we were glad we'd done it. Far away down the corridor, we could see the bodies parting a fraction and could hear a different pattern of feet. Marching! With furtive glances we could see four soldiers rapidly approaching.

They were definitely walking with their heads up: eyes on the lookout all the time. The instinct to run was almost unbearable but the reaction of those around us helped. They did not change pace, but moved away from the four towards the walls, looking, if anything, closer at the floor than before.

We did the same and they passed by in a flash. Round about there were little sighs. We hadn't been the only ones holding their breath.

Although this was a prison we hadn't seen any cells. We had been tramping the seemingly endless corridors for forty-five minutes by now and hadn't found any clues as to where our parents might be. We had given ourselves an hour and then we were going to follow my suggestion of finding the dungeons. Solo was sceptical, but my theory was that they had been built to stop prisoners escaping, so why wouldn't they be used now?

Then, ahead of us, appeared something I had never seen in real life before but recognised from the old video movies. A hospital trolley, being pushed by two nurses. The trolley was occupied but the patient was so wrapped up that it was impossible to see whether they were male or female, or even if they were dead or alive. This time the people around us actually flattened themselves against the wall and looked away when the trolley passed. I glanced at their faces, some of which were full of fear and horror. Did they know what had happened to the patient? Were they frightened it might happen to them?

The trolley stopped by a lift and most of the people swarmed past. Solo collided with me and so we stopped as well. I looked at her questioningly, as best I could with downcast eyes, but she looked at the floor.

Great, I thought, she wants us to get in the lift with that, with them. We'll be noticed immediately.

Fortunately a handful of other people needed to go in the same lift and huddled as far away from the trolley as they could. We joined the huddle.

The body on the trolley began to twitch.

I watched in fascinated horror as the person struggled to become conscious and the white blanket fell away. A nurse tried to throw the blanket back but she was jammed at the far end of the trolley. A shock of curly black hair disentangled itself from the pillow. It was a woman. She moaned.

It was Mum.

# CHAPTER 12

Tears streamed down my face but I couldn't do anything otherwise it would give us away. I looked across at Solo to see if she had noticed me, if I could somehow let her know.

She wasn't looking at me. Tears streaming down her face, she was also looking at the woman on the trolley with agonised recognition.

This wasn't making sense. How could she know my mum? Solo and I had only known each other for the last three or four days!

The lift stopped and everyone followed the trolley out. By now the blanket had been carefully restored but Mum was still thrashing about.

'Let's get her back to M9,' one of the nurses said curtly and they turned the trolley and swiftly pushed it away from us.

Not wanting to lose sight of it we hurried after,

but it was evident that people in green uniforms were a small minority here. Most people were in white coats; quite a few others dressed as nurses. There were far fewer people on this floor too. We could very quickly become conspicuous.

We both saw the door labelled 'Laundry' at the same time and, after looking all round, glided in. It turned out to be a cupboard. This meant it was a very tight squeeze. On the other hand there was no danger of finding anyone else there. And now the door was closed it was pitch black.

'That was my mum, Solo,' I cried. 'What have they done to her?'

Solo sobbed 'It can't be! That was my mum, Sam!'

We hugged each other, letting it go on for a long minute. We didn't understand what we had seen, it was weird. But what we had to do hadn't changed. Solo flicked on a tiny flashlight she'd found somewhere on her – she'd probably be able to rustle up some kindling if she was asked – and we found that fortunately we were in a clean laundry cupboard.

Seconds later we were back out of the cupboard, in clean white coats, blending with the background again, we hoped, and on the trail of the trolley, or room M9, which ever came sooner. Despite the terrible sight in the lift, we felt energised. At least whosever this Mum turned out to be, was alive. One down, three to go.

But, as suddenly as it had gone right for us, just as suddenly it all went wrong.

Up ahead, the trolley had stopped. A white-coated figure who looked like a doctor, was taking over from the nurses. She had her back to us. As we approached, she heard us and turned. For a millisecond her expression was of shock and disbelief.

We turned and walked purposefully in the opposite direction. But not before we had been recognised.

'Get them!' shouted the hateful voice, last heard talking to our captors, as we lay quivering in the secret compartment of the horse truck.

It was Lucy.

If we'd wanted a quick way of finding our parents we'd found one. In seconds we'd been grabbed by our elbows, pushed behind Lucy with the trolley, through a door marked M9 and shoved in. Stumbling into the centre of the room we steadied ourselves and stopped.

The sight that met us made no sense at all.

There were four hospital beds, all occupied except for one – the trolley patient's, obviously. Three people struggled to sit up. One was definitely my mum, so who was still on the trolley? I ran over to her and hugged her. The other two were my dad! Both had straight gingery blond hair like brushes. Both had Solo's green eyes. That couldn't be right, either! I felt queasy, convinced I was seeing things. I could see Solo was having the same problem.

Before anyone could speak, Lucy sneered,

'Oh it's been a real treat watching you trip about the castle, lighting up our security matrix like a set of Christmas tree lights. And now you've done my job for me, all gathered together nicely. You've even identified your own mother. Thank you very much, the pair of you.'

There was a moan from the prisoners as they realised Solo and I had been captured.

I boiled over. I rushed at her and had got a foot on her before anyone could move.

'You traitor!' I screamed, 'You pretended to be our friend, you made us trust you and you betrayed us!'

Somewhere else I could hear another fight going on. Solo had attacked a guard. But it all ended in less than thirty seconds when Lucy pushed me violently to the floor.

'Don't you ever try anything like that again you little fool,' she snarled. 'Get her up,' she ordered the guards. 'You really are quite full of yourselves, aren't you?' She looked at me pityingly. 'You gave yourselves away,' she said. 'Your foolish dog made it very obvious and then your body heat showed up on the heatseeker.'

Oh Vince. I had known that really.

Lucy barked out an order and she and the guards left. The door slammed behind them.

Then the woman on the trolley turned towards me. I could tell now, close to, she wasn't Mum. Extremely like her, but not.

She cleared her throat and spoke with difficulty. 'Are you . . . are you . . . ?' But the effort was too much and anyway, Solo rushed to her.

'Mum, Mum, what have they done to you?' she cried.

Why were all our parents locked up in the same room?

'Your parents, my parents,' I said carefully, 'they all look the same. Are they clones or something?'

There was a weak murmur from the other beds. Apparently they all had humungous headaches from the truth drugs and they had no desire to sit upright yet.

'Look,' said the man who was not my dad, 'we've not got much time. Now they've found you both . . .'

I'd been struggling, but suddenly I knew that voice! I'd spoken to it lots of times on the radio.

'You're Vince's brother!' I declared.

'That's correct,' he said, 'we meet in person!'

'I thought it wasn't your voice on the radio,' I said anxiously, 'but we did all the right passwords and he sent me to Ron. I hope I didn't give you away . . .' I trailed off, suddenly haunted by the thought that I'd played into the hands of the enemy. Was it actually Ron who was the traitor?

'No, no Tamsin,' my dad reassured me, 'everything went as it should.'

'We're very proud of you honey,' said Mum. 'You remembered <u>everything</u>. All the practice was worth it . . .'

'Except it's got us here. And we should have stayed away, shouldn't we? No help at all,' I said flatly.

'Tamsin, we've got two more chances of help than we had before,' said Dad. He was always so positive. I hugged him.

'Okay,' butted in Solo. 'Help me here. I've got two identical guys one of which is my dad and two identical women . . .'

'All right, all right.' It was my mum. 'This is my sister, Helena. As you can probably see, we are identical twins. She is older than me by fifteen minutes which she never stops reminding me of. We met your fathers at university where we were studying Biomedical Sciences. As you see, they are also identical twins. This apparently is not uncommon, especially with identical twins. It takes a twin to understand a twin.'

'Quite,' said my dad and uncle, together.

'They were both doing something in computers, which we never understood, did we Helena?'

'No,' said Helena, weakly.

'We fell in love, got married, had babies and were all set to live happily ever after . . .'

'When a bunch of dictators took over,' continued Dad, 'and you know the rest.'

'But hundreds of thousands of people, like us, were starting to be rounded up and imprisoned.' My uncle was speaking now. 'And people had been killed, even though it was said to be a bloodless coup.'

'The king was killed,' I put in. Dad had told me that as well.

'Not only the king,' replied my uncle, 'but his wife, their sons and daughters, grandchildren and great grandchildren. A massacre of nearly one hundred people. The whole royal family.'

'Or so they thought,' Mum said. 'But they hadn't done their homework. There were two people, cousins to one of the great grandchildren, who they had forgotten. Those people were now the next-in-line.'

'Who were they?' I breathed.

'Me and your mum!' It was Helena. I could hardly believe my ears.

'Yes. I am the Queen now,' she said.

I was in shock. Not only did I now have a family twice as big as before, but my aunt was the Queen!

'Are you the king?' I whispered to my uncle.

'No, I'm not,' he replied, 'if I was anything, I'd be the consort.'

'But that means that Solo is, I mean my cousin is . . . a princess! You never told me you were a princess!' I accused Solo.

'Of course I didn't! A – you thought I was a boy,' she smirked and I blushed, 'and B – you never asked. But C – I've only just found out myself! And D – *You* never told me *you* were a princess, Sam!'

I hadn't thought it through, but she was right. And Mum as well of course.

'Honestly Mum,' Solo said, exasperated now, 'Very Important, High Up on the Wanted List! That's what you told me. Never mentioned being the Queen!'

'It's not the title that's important,' said Helena quietly. 'We didn't even tell your fathers when we first met. Being one hundred and something in line for the throne was nothing to shout about, when the rest of the family was still alive. But suddenly, the right to choose how we're governed had been stolen from us. The monarchy and the Queen became the banner behind which the Resistance mustered. When I was asked I only accepted with reluctance. Then suddenly I became number one on the wanted list. We've managed to keep one step ahead of them for fourteen years,' she finished gloomily.

'Why didn't you hide in the country like Mum and Dad?' I wanted to know.

There was a short silence.

'We wanted to . . . er . . . spread the risk,' my uncle said after a pause. 'One of us would go underground—'

'And the other would go on the run,' finished my dad.

Solo and I stared at each other. 'Like decoys,' we breathed together. The adults hadn't heard.

I was still puzzled. 'How did they find the Pad, after all this time? Somebody must have betrayed us!'

There was silence.

'Of course they did,' said Helena, finally.

'It was us! Your uncle and I betrayed you!'

# CHAPTER 13

Solo and I stood aghast, but my parents were unmoved.

'We betrayed you because they caught us first and gave us the drugs. After that, no-one at the top of the Tube was safe.'

I turned to Mum and Dad. 'You're at the top of the Tube?' I demanded.

How could they be? Nothing much ever went on other than the short regular radio calls. Just shows how much I knew.

Dad must have read my mind. 'I'm Communications Co-ordinator for my sins. Your uncle's Operations.'

There was so much to take in. The four adults were starting to feel less queasy so got up. My cousin Solo was apparently called Beatrice but real names were a rarity round here. I had never known my parents' first names; my uncle was still

'Vince's brother' to me and Helena – was that really her name? We all looked at each other for a long moment.

It was getting embarrassing.

'What happened to your hair, girls?' asked Mum.

We gave them a quick explanation and I told them that Oscar and Vince were still with Ron. Dad buried his face in his hands.

'I thought Vince must have been burnt to death,' he sobbed. I hugged him again.

'Who's Ron?' asked Mum sharply.

Solo explained how he ran a horse troupe that was more than it seemed.

'We may know him by another name,' said Helena.

I'd been watching my new family.

'Solo, you're so like my dad, you know. You've got the same curl of the lip when you're being sarcastic!'

'Gee thanks Sam. And your eyes are just the exact same colour as my mum's. Must be the twin thing' she quipped, 'that one where you take after your uncle or aunt more than your mum and dad!'

'So I wasn't born in Cornwall after all,' I said, thoughtfully, thinking back to the conversation. 'So am I not Tamsin either?'

Another little silence.

But then, with a sudden clarity, I had it all. Or thought I had.

'Oscar was your horse, wasn't he?' I asked Helena. 'And you did lots of trick riding with him. It was you who taught him how to do it!' I turned to my parents. 'It was obvious that he was teaching me, and not the other way round!' And then I mortified myself by blubbing. 'I miss him so much . . .'

Helena hugged me.

'That makes two of us. Every time I ride a horse, I think of him.'

'Look, girls.' My dad now, suddenly urgent. 'Whatever happens, however hard, you two must escape! Never mind us! Leave us! It is imperative you get out!'

'No way!' Solo protested. 'We've got this far . . .'

There was a noise, the door opened and four soldiers, each carrying a rifle, marched in.

'Right yer stoopid majesty, we're off,' the leader rudely shouted into Helena's face. 'All get into line, now!'

The adults looked terrible. They were all in white hospital gowns, which made them look ghostly pale. They were bent and unsteady on their feet and looked about ninety.

'Where are we going?' demanded Helena, with an effort.

'Dungeons,' said the leader, 'firing squad.' A man of few words.

My mum moaned and half fainted. We caught her.

'Get into line. Querwick march!' ordered the leader, undeterred.

I looked at Solo who shook her head. We were definitely not leaving without them.

'What's happening here?' Lucy had appeared again. For some reason she looked a little dishevelled, her cheeks flushed. She took a quick look around as if counting us all.

'Orders are, take them to the dungeon, prepare for firing squad, ma'am.' This time the leader showed respect.

Lucy pulled herself up to her full height and bellowed

'Let's get on with it then!' and led us out.

I hated her.

There were five of them, six of us but the way our parents were shuffling along, weak limbed and muzzy headed, the odds were stacked in their favour. What sort of treatment had turned my extremely fit mum and dad into physical wrecks in such a short time? And how on earth would they be able to get enough energy to escape, if the opportunity arose?

As before, all eyes were averted as our little

party passed. Where was the rescue party which Solo's people had promised her? Were we it?

Finally, we made it into a lift where the adults leant against the walls, totally spent. Solo raised her eyebrows at me, obviously having the same thoughts.

On exiting the lift at Floor D (for Dungeons?) the guards moved us to the left and halted by a door labelled D3. Bristling with metal straps it had a meshed spy window at face height. To get in there was a push button pad. One-way only then.

'Why are you stopping here?' barked Lucy.

'Our orders is D3 ma'am,' responded the leader.

'My orders are D5,' Lucy insisted haughtily. 'You obviously heard wrongly.' There was a bead of sweat dripping off the end of her nose.

'I did no . . . sorry ma'am. Forward march!' the leader corrected, suddenly remembering he was outranked.

We stopped again, outside D5. Lucy punched the code and we all went in.

Slamming the door behind her Lucy immediately started taunting Solo and me again, calling us a pair of losers, sneering at us trying to pass as boys, how it would be a real pleasure for her to watch our execution minutes from now.

Her face was so close to mine that I could feel the spit from her lips. We couldn't do anything; we were outmatched in strength and weapons. I was getting really wound up again.

Suddenly she grabbed me and swung me round. Now she had her back to everyone else. She continued to taunt me, stabbing at me with a forefinger, pushing me further away from the group. Suddenly, with a quick flick, she thrust her face into mine and hissed, so that only I could hear,

'Kick me!'

Then she spat in my face.

Like an enraged bull I went at her and kicked her in the neck.

She went down like a stone.

Over her shoulder Solo was on the move. The guards were running forward and she kicked one in the neck also and he followed Lucy down. Dad managed to trip one just by sticking his foot out at the perfect moment, but he wasn't staying down. As he arose, Mum, who had found a rifle, hit him with it and down he went again.

Three down, two to go. These two were now facing us with rifles pointed and one was struggling to get at his radio with one hand.

'Splits!' ordered my uncle. Fortunately we'd been trained by identical twins. I'd played it in fun before, as a child, giggling as Dad tried to catch Mum or me. Now it was for our lives as we all threw ourselves to the floor, splitting in six different directions to distract the soldiers, who didn't know where to point.

Helena got to one first, grabbing at his knees to try and bring him down. She was so weak it was pathetic. He raised his rifle to shoot her, but suddenly realising who it was, hesitated. He must have needed an order to kill the top prisoner. That gave Solo the split second she needed to leap up into his face, take a good hold of his jacket, turn in and throw him and his rifle over her shoulder and down. She went over and started to tie him up while my uncle stuffed one of the soldier's own socks in his mouth to keep him quiet.

Meanwhile Dad and I had managed to bring the leader down, but in a very messy fashion, of which we were not proud. The main objective was to shut him and his radio up. He was extremely strong and seemed to object to the sock in the mouth treatment, so Mum came and hit him with the rifle after which he went very quiet.

All five down – but had we gained anything?

We were in a large room with stone walls, a high ceiling and a heavily fortified door. In other words – a dungeon. It was fairly gloomy, with no lights. But it wasn't pitch black.

So there must be some natural light coming from somewhere. The brothers were trying to work out from where.

'I think it's from there, where the wall and the ceiling meet,' said my uncle, pointing.

'Is it a skylight?' asked Mum.

'We won't know until we look,' said Dad.

So we all stood and looked. At least five metres above us in a completely empty room, was a tantalising strip of light, which may or may not have been — what?

'Okay, okay,' said my uncle briskly. You could tell why he was 'Operations'. ' What we need is erm . . .'

'A ladder?' suggested Helena.

'That's right, a ladder.'

If it wasn't so deadly serious, it would have been funny. Any minute the door would be blown in and we were for the firing squad.

'We could do a ladder, eh Sam?' said Solo, thinking, as always, on her feet. Or with her feet.

'That would take us just over halfway,' I calculated, shrugging.

There was a pause, as greater minds than ours took over.

'What d'you think? Could we do it for a few minutes?' Dad asked his twin.

'No argument. We've got to.' But his voice sounded so frail success seemed unlikely.

But he jammed his back against the wall, cupped his hands and flexed his wobbling knees. Dad stepped onto his hands and painfully climbed up his poor brother's chest onto his shoulders. That made my uncle fall forward but Helena and Mum pushed him back and leaned against him to give him support.

I could have cried. Whenever we practised this, Mum and Dad were always much better at it than I was – so agile and strong . . .

'You next, carrot top,' shouted my uncle. Only a dad would get away with that.

I was going last. Solo reckoned I was lighter than her. Made no difference – someone had to.

I went up like it was a real ladder and when I got there I forgot myself and shrieked so loudly that we almost tumbled like a house of cards.

'It's a window! And guess what? It's open!'

'Tell the world, why don't you?' hissed Solo. She was right of course.

'Open! Could we get through?' whispered Mum.

'Yes! We could squeeze. But there is one teeny problem.'

'Oh yeah, what's that?'

'There are iron bars across it.'

Well, it was a dungeon.

'What's outside?' asked Dad.

'It looks like it's at street level,' I said. 'Not a main road, not lots of people, but I can hear traffic.'

'What about calling for help?' asked Dad.

'We could send for help,' burst in Solo. 'Look, Rosemary'll get help!'

'ROSEMARY?' asked five people in unison. We'd completely forgotten Rosemary.

'I hid her in your bed Mum,' explained Solo simply. 'I thought they might search us when they caught us.'

'Oh, good darling,' said Helena faintly.

'What on earth can she do?' I asked.

'Stands to reason Lucy set this up, yes? She didn't let you kick her for fun. So hopefully she'll have someone out there ready and waiting. For a signal.' She passed the rat up to me.

I wished I had her optimism as I pushed Rosemary through the bars and out of the window. With a little squeak she was off, scuttling along the pavement at my eye level. If this didn't work we'd be facing a firing squad and neither of us would be seeing our pets again.

The men felt they could stand for five minutes, to give it a chance. When five minutes were up, the ladder started to dismantle. Just then, I thought

I heard a noise, and asked for another couple of seconds.

It was a noise, but one I wasn't expecting. As it came nearer it sounded like a pig snuffling at a trough. Then whatever it was sounded like they were clicking on knitting needles along the pavement. Then it became a whimper, then a whine then an excited explosion of yelps.

Then a big black and white head thrust itself through the bars and tried to lick my hand off.

# CHAPTER 14

Hot on the heels of the ecstatic Vince came a familiar grumble.

'Will someone shut that stupid hound up! He'll give us all away – again!'

'Oh, but he found us, didn't he Ron?' I tried to laugh. It was more a choke. I was trying not to cry.

'Are you all in there?' Ron queried, trying to see in.

'Yes, but we can't hold this much longer,' I said desperately. I could feel the ladder shifting, ready to crumble.

'Get down,' ordered Ron. 'I've got all the equipment ready. Now I know where you are we can get started.' He turned to go.

'How are you going to get through the bars?' I asked him.

He laughed. 'How d'you think. Grapple hooks and horses! Now get down!'

'Ron says he's going to get grapple hooks and horses,' I explained, as I jumped off the collapsing 'ladder'. Solo jumped at the same time as the two men slid to the floor, groaning and rubbing their shoulders.

'He's kidding you,' said Helena, who was giving my uncle a shoulder massage. 'Grapple hooks and horses wouldn't move steel rods! This is a dungeon.'

'He'll be getting some steel cutting stuff,' said my uncle, knowledgeably.

'Again, I doubt it,' persisted Helena. 'Those bars will be linked to an alarm system.'

She was right of course. But would Ron know this? And even if he did, what other options were there?

'I'd rather die trying to get out, than in front of a firing squad,' said Solo.

And she spoke for all of us.

Ron was on the ball. Through the bars he thrust an assorted collection of clothes and told everybody to get changed – there was work to do!

'As soon as we touch these bars, the alarms will go,' he said, confirming Helena's belief. 'So let's have as many of you as we can up the top here, before we start.'

As he spoke, he threw down a rope ladder

which, he assured us, was tied securely to the horse wagon and would take all of us at once.

As the ladder snaked down to us, my heart lifted. For the first time since we'd been captured, I started to believe we could get out. We'd be up there as quick as anything, easy peasy.

The next second however, our prospects seemed blacker than ever. Before the bars had even been touched, the door was being battered. Two soldiers groaned, reminding us that they were still a threat. But the worst thing was the bleak reception of the rope ladder by our parents.

I'd forgotten how weak they were. Normally they'd have chased to the top. Not now. Now they were defeated. They didn't even make the first rung.

We could hear Ron and others above, getting the cutting equipment ready. In a minute, he'd start, expecting us to be ready to pile out as soon as the gap was big enough.

'You and Beatrice go.' The conversation we had started hours ago, resumed.

'No!' we both said. 'All or nothing,' I added for good luck.

'I'm commanding you,' said Helena, as regally as she could.

'No, Mum. No your majesty,' Solo and I said together.

We weren't getting anywhere. Any of us.

Solo swung up the ladder like a monkey and out of earshot had a few words with Ron. She scrambled down again.

The banging on the door had stopped. Not good news, Dad said, they'd be bringing reinforcements.

'This is what we do,' she said. 'Mums will go up to there,' she pointed a few rungs up. 'Sam and I'll come and hold you on. Dads will have to climb up a couple each and hang on as best they can.'

Suddenly a high pitched screeching noise started, then a thud, as Ron's cutting equipment dug into the first bar. The castle alarms immediately set off and penetrating sirens filled our ears.

'Get in position. Ron will pull us up,' Solo yelled. 'We'll end up black and blue, but we won't be dead!'

She had started to help Helena onto the rope. That was the correct order. Queen and Princess Number One, first. Once we could get onto the first rung, I did the same with my mum.

Immediately we were on I could feel a tug. We started to rise.

'We're not all on!' I screamed, 'stop!'

'She can't climb any more,' shouted Solo, 'we'll come back for them!'

The ladder bumped and banged against the wall, our hands taking the brunt of it.

Below the penetrating alarms and cutting equipment a low, rhythmic noise had started. I could see the cell door shuddering with each beat and knew it would only be seconds.

'Get the guns!' I yelled down at the men, but they were way ahead of me and were already armed, backed up to the wall, covering the ladder.

The screeching above suddenly stopped and the ladder accelerated upwards. As Helena and Solo approached the window I felt a weight below us, looked down and saw that my uncle had managed to get a foot on the very bottom rung. He was struggling to hold on, his face crimson with the effort.

The door burst open and then the shooting began.

Above me Helena and Solo had reached the window and hands were hauling Helena through the gap.

The Queen was safe. Princess Number One had other plans.

Swinging down she suddenly was level with me.

'Go back!' I shouted. 'Your dad's on the ladder!' I could still feel his weight.

'So?' she said.

There was a thunderous burst of gunfire and a scream of agony.

'Oh no!' Mum moaned and lost her grip. But she was caught and hauled, sobbing, through the window.

Hand over hand we climbed down past my uncle, still clinging on. Somehow he'd managed to hang onto the gun as well.

'Go Dad!' Solo shouted.

I couldn't make out my dad at first. We leapt down into chaos. There were wounded soldiers everywhere, some were struggling up, some frighteningly still. The leader was getting to his feet methodically, not rushing: checking what was happening after each move. He was dangerous.

Then I saw Dad, or at least his arm. It was the only one not in green and there was a large red patch on it which was getting bigger as I watched. Preventing me from seeing the rest of him was another body on top. With a shock, I recognised Lucy. She must have recovered and leapt on him after he was shot while covering us on the ladder. She was protecting him! But had she been shot too?

No! She looked round carefully before slowly starting to get up. She found her rifle, then she saw us. She looked the other way.

Dad had rolled over and was trying to get up.

'I don't think I can walk,' he whispered through gritted teeth.

'Put your arms round us,' I said and we lifted him up as gently as we could and started for the wall. The ladder had dropped down again for us and we half lifted, half dragged him towards it. He was so heavy I knew he must be only just conscious. We were agonisingly close when Lucy came up alongside. Her rifle was pointing at us.

'So near and yet so far,' she sneered. She was actually looking over my shoulder and I turned to look. There, aiming his rifle at us as well was the careful leader. We were caught in the middle, with no way out. We held our breath, waiting for the inevitable.

Lucy fired, but not at us! Instead she had fired over my shoulder. The leader was down. 'I'll cover you! Go!' Lucy cried, ducking around us and letting off a volley of bullets. More people came streaming through the door, many wearing balaclavas! The Tube rescue force – at last?

We took advantage and, with Dad between us, heaved ourselves onto the first rung. Immediately, we started to ascend, every second expecting to be hit by a bullet. Below, a battle raged once more and it was impossible to tell who was taking part and for whom.

Lucy had her back to the wall we were climbing. She was still covering us as we rose. As our feet came level with her head she was hit. She jerked with the force of it, then slumped forward.

'Tell Her Majesty . . .' she choked, then slid to the floor.

Without Lucy we were totally exposed. A huge target moving too slowly up the wall. Once again we braced ourselves for the inevitable.

A new stream of bullets burst over our heads, but downwards from above! Someone up there was coolly, steadily and accurately providing us with an umbrella of fire under which we could climb.

We were at the window. Strong hands grabbed Dad and pulled him through, blood pouring down his back from his shoulder. Mum threw down the rifle and sank down too, cradling Dad's head in her arms on the pavement.

'This has got to stop,' came his muffled voice.

'I know. I know,' she sobbed.

'Into the wagon, usual place,' ordered Ron. 'We'll look at the wound on the move, if you don't mind,' he said to Dad. 'I'd rather not do a hospital visit in Newchester if we can help it!'

Mum picked up the rifle and resumed strafing duty. Now it was Solo's turn. She didn't need any help and clambered up and pulled herself through the window. As I stepped up to the last rung I caught a glimpse of the nondescript farm wagon waiting to take us to freedom. In the shafts, two ordinary looking beasts, tacked up like farm horses, stamping their feet. I knew their fit, muscled bodies were poised, ready for flight. They would gallop to hell and back for us if they were asked. One of them was . . .

'Oscar!' I yelled. He whinnied his special greeting to me, one ear swivelled in my direction.

There was a shout from below. Reinforcements had arrived which produced a volley of fire with a different sound – deeper, heavier.

'C'mon Sam,' urged Solo, 'you're there, you're there!'

Their hands were on my arms. My feet had started to leave the rope. There was a huge explosion. The impact when it hit me jolted me off the ladder. There was a brief moment when I felt I was disintegrating around my left knee.

I fell, gratefully escaping the agony into blissful black unconsciousness.

# CHAPTER 15

From the deepest black to brilliant white. I found myself staring into the brightest light I had ever seen. Then I couldn't and had to screw up my eyes against it. From behind the lamp a voice: Dad's. In the background, women were sobbing.

'Sam,' Dad said, 'you're going to be all right, honey.' Why was Dad calling me Sam? 'We're at a vet's who Ron knows. He's in the Tube and he's. .he's going to sort your leg out.'

His voice cracked and the black shape behind the lamp changed. A different voice now, one I didn't recognise.

'Hi Sam,' it said, brisk and to the point. 'Your left leg was smashed beyond repair from the knee down. We have just about stopped the bleeding but I'm afraid you're going to lose your leg from below the knee.'

It wasn't a surprise. The memory of the injury was excruciating, or was that just the pain now? Let's get it over. But—

'A vet? Horse vets don't usually do amputations,' I protested weakly.

'No, they usually shoot their patients instead,' responded the vet drily. The background sobbing increased. 'Just try to imagine me as an orthopaedic surgeon who saw a career changing opportunity in the equine world.'

So he'd had to run once too. And now was risking his life, helping me.

'Will I have to bite on something hard, or drink a gallon of rum?' I asked, remembering my history lessons and the gory accounts of operations long ago. The sobbing changed to a choking wail.

'C'mon Mrs Farmer, you'll be in no fit state to act as anaesthetist,' the vet chided. 'And fortunately for you Sam, I have a little bit of, how should I put it, contraband stuff which will knock you out quite satisfactorily.'

Anything to get rid of the pain. But now, people were appearing round the light. Mum first, her eyes all red, in a white coat, hair covered and mask on. She blew a kiss and disappeared back round my head end. Dad next, chucked my chin and hurried away. Helena and my uncle came then – were they all saying goodbye? – but it didn't matter. Let's do it.

Solo was bending over me. She was the only one who was smiling – but even that looked a bit fixed for her.

'I always wanted a sister,' she started.

'But all you'll have is three quarters of a cousin,' I finished.

She mock punched me and we clasped hands.

'Where's Vince?' I remember asking.

Mum had put a mask over my face and the vet said,

'The last thing I heard was that he is underneath y. . .'

And that was the last thing I heard, too.

Minutes/hours/days? later I woke to an argument going on round my bed.

'We didn't want you anywhere near Newchester at all!' my uncle was saying loudly.

'Trust you two to get together!' added Helena, 'if you hadn't, you probably wouldn't have attempted it on your own.'

'And you would all be dead!' said Solo vehemently.

There was no answer to that.

So I said 'Hello,' very quietly into the silence and enjoyed the reaction.

After a few minutes of fussing, and Vince had been allowed on my bed at my head end away from the tent over my amputation, which I decided not to look at for the minute, everyone settled down again. It was as though we were having a party.

'Apparently Lucy was a double agent,' Solo told me.

'That's some sort of a spy, isn't it?' I asked.

'She spied for us, but pretended she was on their side,' explained Helena. 'There are hundreds like her, risking their lives every minute, for freedom.'

A man with a mask came in to check on me and as soon as I heard his voice I recognised the vet. He was going to remain anonymous he told me, but I noticed he was not looking at my face either. It seemed I was well enough to move and that must be done as soon as possible for his sake and ours.

'It will hurt Sam,' he said gently, 'but you are young and it will heal quickly. I look forward to working with a real horse next time – perhaps one of yours?' He squeezed my shoulder.

I could feel the tears welling up and looked away. It had been my blackest fear that I would never be able to ride again. And he had known. Then he said his goodbyes and left.

The room began filling with people, all masked and gowned – for hygiene or disguise? Probably both. Still woozy, I fell asleep again and next time I awoke properly we were in another room. This time it was light and airy, the noises beneath us sounding as though we were above a flock of chickens!

'Spot on Holmes,' joked my dad, 'we are in a secret room above an egg production plant. Even you can't make more noise than all those chickens!' I struggled to sit up. The pain was excruciating but so was my back from lying down so long. So hard luck. Once upright, the nausea passed.

'Don't tell your mother,' he whispered, nodding to the gently snoring figure splayed on a bed of straw at the foot of my bed. 'You're not supposed to be sitting up until tomorrow.'

'I guess she'll notice eventually,' I said. 'Dad, what's going to happen about the Pad? And Primrose and Peony and Petunia? (our jersey cows) and . . .'

Dad put his hand up to halt me.

'We can't go back. It's over. We've done very well to remain hidden for so long. The others the same. You two have proved more than capable of looking after yourselves. We have entered the final phase in this war.'

This man bore no resemblance to the white frail patient of two days ago, nor to the laid back one paced farmer who had patiently taught me. This man had a steely determination and a glitter in his eye.

'Final phase?'

'Yes. The restoration of freedom. Behind the banner of monarchy, if we must.'

Oh, that's all.

'Going back to the cows.' I must have been so weak that the thought of never seeing those beautiful docile animals or my naughty escaping sheep again was making me blub!

Dad hugged me. Actually, we both needed a handkerchief. Sudden onset of dust from below. We blew our noses thoroughly.

'Hon,' whispered Dad, 'imagine all that, without having to zigzag home so you're not followed, or jump in a bush every time a helicopter comes over. I promise that to you. In the meantime, I'm sure the animals can go next door.'

Our neighbours' farm, a mile away. I'd never met them, but their animals shared our common moor and they were as sleek and healthy as ours. Our animals, the only friends I'd ever known. I'd needed to know there was a plan for them in our future as well.

Solo appeared with a chicken sandwich.

'Fancy one?' she laughed.

'I'd rather have a hog roast.'

Later Solo said, 'I don't understand. If Lucy was a double agent, why couldn't she just let you out?'

'There were four of us,' explained Dad, 'and you saw the state we were in. She would have needed help.' Then he looked at the others.

'We'd all expected help,' explained Helena. 'We know that in the Castle alone, there are at least four hundred Tube members working undercover!'

'Four hundred?' Solo and I echoed.

'They should have been able to organise a breakout in the time we had,' Helena continued, 'but nothing happened.'

'Or something happened,' said my uncle grimly.

'We think something's happened at the top of the Tube. Someone must have betrayed our safe house. It's only ever known to a handful of people. That same person made sure you two ended up in Ron's outfit. Then that person prevented the news of our capture getting to the Tube members in the castle. Another double agent,' Helena whispered, 'working for them, this time.'

'Someone like that is known as a Mole,' supplied my uncle, 'and one at the very top. It's one of our most trusted friends, must be.' The others were nodding, thinking. 'And if we don't catch them, it could blow us apart.'

'No wonder Lucy looked shocked when she saw just us two,' commented Solo. 'She must have been expecting the cavalry!'

I'd been thinking. 'I think I've spoken to the Mole.'

'On the radio. Yes, it might have been,' agreed my uncle.

'He told me to go to the Devil's Riders and to stay there. And then there was that nice family,' I faltered.

'They were probably following the Mole's orders in good faith,' my mum put in.

I hoped so. 'They told me to find Ron and he obviously wasn't expecting me,' I remembered.

'Same with me,' agreed Solo.

'If Ron had been expecting you and known who you were, he'd have kept you hidden,' said Helena.

'And he'd probably have turned north, away from Newchester, the minute you both arrived,' Mum agreed.

'But Lucy knew who I was, so the Mole must have told her, thinking she was on their side. She tried her best as the Black Knight to stop me from going to Newchester and to prevent those guards from finding us.'

'Those guards knew exactly what they were looking for – two girls,' said Solo.

'Three targeted raids in four nights,' I added.

It was obvious. He had got us where he wanted us and picked us up, just when he wanted to.

'He's top priority,' said Helena. 'We've got to get him.'

'Or her,' said Mum.

# EPILOGUE

I'm shivering and it's not with cold.

It's with terror.

Anyone ten minutes away from falling out of a small plane on a moonless night has a right to be terrified.

Nathan, my 'buddy' sitting beside me on the bench seat behind the pilot – he's not terrified. He's parachuted 'more times than I've had a pork pie, luv.' Judging by the size of his muscles rippling under his combat shirt and his tree trunk neck, he's had plenty of those. He's so not terrified, he's almost asleep.

Dad wasn't terrified. He's done it before, too. The only concern was his shoulder. Luckily the bullet had gone straight through so no surgery has been required. Vince's quick healing ointment is already doing its magic. We dropped Dad forty minutes ago near the Pad. After sorting out our animals, he'll join up with Mum.

'The Queen and Freedom!' he shouted, falling backwards and away.

Helena and my uncle are not terrified either. It's not in their vocabulary. We're dropping them now near where there is a strong Tube community. They'll set up the new HQ there.

'It's what we do for a living,' says Helena, ruefully.

And then they'll dig out the Mole.

Mum's going with them. When Dad joins her, they're heading across country to where there used to be a military rehabilitation centre. They're hoping it's still there. And that someone there might be able to make me a prosthetic ankle and foot. If they're in the Tube.

Lots of 'ifs' and 'mights 'and 'hopes'. I've added one more: only if I can ride with it. Otherwise I'll make do with the telescopic crutch stowed in my backpack and limp around, crowing 'ah har Jim lad!' Like Long John Silver.

The adults were not amused. Nor were they when Solo and I insisted we could now act as an independent operating unit.

It's our age of course. We're still only fourteen and should be under the safe protection . . . blah de blah. We say, maybe still only fourteen but who, unaided, delivered four of you safely from the teeth of the enemy?

'The Queen and Freedom!' Mum shouts and blows a kiss as she throws herself backwards. She thinks they've won the argument, but they haven't. Because as soon as possible the Last Phase will commence – the battle to overthrow the regime – and they'll need every man, woman, child and animal they can lay their hands on.

Solo's next. She's not terrified, just angry that she's got to have a buddy. She hasn't done enough jumps to be able to jump alone.

'Can't we just stretch a point, considering the circumstances?' she'd challenged her mum. By circumstances she'd meant the stolen plane: the fact that every man, woman and teenager was in full combat gear: the fact that it was a night time, covert operation.

I can see what she meant. But Helena just shook her head, absently, as if Solo had been a toddler asking for matches. At least she can concentrate on not squashing Rosemary when they land.

I am secretly really happy to have the snoring Nathan.

Tightly bound to her buddy Solo waves and beams her big brave smile, shouting

'The Queen and Freedom!' They back out of the plane and disappear. Ron's down there somewhere. He's 'Viktor's Amazing Russian Cossack

Troupe' now. Oscar's never been a Cossack horse before.

Only three of us left to go. My shivering along with the appalling din, intensifies.

Vince isn't terrified. Wearing my ear protectors he's insulated from the noise and happy enough strapped to me in a harness on my lap.

Everyone is worried about me jumping with my newly acquired stump.

'It's a stump,' I say, 'how can it get any worse? By becoming a mangled stump?'

That's why I've got Nathan. He seems to be twice my height and weight. When he stands, with me and Vince strapped round his middle, my feet . . . foot doesn't touch the ground. If we have to go over, he says, he'll make sure he goes over backwards so that we don't land on Vince. That's my real fear.

Seconds to go. Nathan, suddenly alert, slides up close, lifts Vince and me up like two feathers and clips us to his harness. We make it to the door and get into position, facing inwards.

Of course we didn't do it all on our own. We couldn't have done any of it without brave, brave Lucy. Helena says that when it's all over, courageous people like Lucy will be honoured. But Lucy wasn't her real name, so how will we know . . . ?

The pilot shouts. It's time.

'Ten, nine, eight. .' I count down with Nathan, as he's taught me.

'Five, four, three, two, one, JUMP!'

'The Queen and Freedom!' we both shout as he pushes out.

Names. Am I Tamsin? Is she Beatrice? Why does Solo look so much like my Dad? Why am I the image of Helena? The questions tumble with me, in me.

The speed is sensational and, now the plane has gone, the silence thrilling. I wish it was daylight! I want to see! But Vince is shaking.

Too soon the parachute opens with a silky slither and a crack and we are jolted upright.

'It's brilliant,' I squeal, 'I've got to do this again!'

'Thought so,' Nathan laughs, 'but silence now. We'll be heard.'

Stately and controlled, we lose height. Hopefully in a field near a church, Ron who is now Viktor and Oscar will meet us with the farm wagon and take Vince, Rosemary, Solo and me to the Cossacks. I can't wait to sit behind my sturdy friend again and watch his exquisite comma ears point our way there.

Tamsin/Sam. Beatrice/Solo. Ron/Viktor. Uncle. Dad. Queen Helena. Mum. Lucy. Oscar. Vince, Rosemary.

Safely down to earth again with a soft crumple – back in the warzone.

## Acknowledgements

Sue H, North Norfolk Writers; Aki and team at The Literary Consultancy, for all your encouragement and belief in this; Lucy at Head & Heart for steering me through the process.

## About the Author

Anne Olivant now lives in beautiful North Norfolk after having lived in the equally beautiful Cornwall. Here she shares her life with a mixture of human, furry and feathered friends, her children and their families. Amongst other things she is a writer, teacher and carer. She loves to walk and cycle in the surrounding countryside and, if she could find a horse to share, she would be riding around it as well!

Lightning Source UK Ltd.
Milton Keynes UK
UKOW01f0709230717
305834UK00001B/11/P